"And I want to know what in the name of hell you're gonna do about it." Hostility radiated from Bubba Gibson. "My animals ain't supposed to drop dead, Manny. They're supposed to be healthy. *You* checked them. Now they're dead!"

"At this point, I don't have any answers," Manny said.

"Well, I'm tired of my future dyin' on me. Every time you stop by, something bad happens. And I ain't gonna stand for it no more."

"Are you trying to say something, Bubba?" Manny asked with a menacing quietness.

"I'm bringing in a veterinarian from Austin to look at the cattle and make sure there wasn't anything else you missed on your routine visits that will cost me a fortune. You see, Manny, I ain't *trying* to tell you nothin'. I *am* tellin' you that we won't be requirin' your services no more. And I'll be spreading the word to my friends, too."

Special thanks and acknowledgment to Kathy Clark
for her contribution to the Crystal Creek series.

Special thanks and acknowledgment to Sutton Press Inc.
for its contribution to the concept for the Crystal Creek series.

ISBN 0-373-82522-6

STAND BY YOUR MAN

Stand By Your Man

Kathy Clark

Harlequin Books

TORONTO • NEW YORK • LONDON
AMSTERDAM • PARIS • SYDNEY • HAMBURG
STOCKHOLM • ATHENS • TOKYO • MILAN
MADRID • WARSAW • BUDAPEST • AUCKLAND

Dear Reader,

"Harlequin's new special series called Crystal Creek wonderfully evokes the hot days and steamy nights of a small Texas community... impossible to put down until the last page is turned."

—Romantic Times

If this is your first visit to Crystal Creek, come meet veterinarian Manny Hernandez... and the McKinneys, the Randolphs and the Gibsons—just a few of the folks who live, love and ranch in the small Texas Hill Country community of Crystal Creek. And if you're returning for more of the linked stories you love, you won't be disappointed with the romances some of your favorite authors still have in store for you! Barbara Kaye, Margot Dalton, Bethany Campbell, Sharon Brondos, Kathy Clark and Cara West have created wonderful tales with a true Texas flavor and all the elements you've come to expect in your romance reading: compelling, contemporary characters caught in conflicts that reflect today's dilemmas.

And there's great news! Many readers have written to tell us that, once immersed in Crystal Creek, it's hard to leave. Well, now you don't have to! The terrific popularity of this series has prompted us to bring twelve additional Crystal Creek titles your way! The series will continue with more wonderful romances created by the authors who first brought Crystal Creek to life, and Penny Richards and Sandy Steen will also be contributing new novels and characters to the continuing saga of Crystal Creek. Watch for them every month, wherever Harlequin books are sold.

Stick around in Crystal Creek—home of sultry Texas drawls, smooth Texas charm and tall, sexy Texans!

Marsha Zinberg
Coordinator, Crystal Creek

A Note from the Author

When I was a little girl growing up in Alvin, Texas, I used to ride my horse all day and dream of becoming a veterinarian. I always thought vets had one of the best jobs in the world, until I realized they have to deal with more than delivering spindly legged foals and giving rabies shots to fuzzy little puppies. I decided I didn't want to face the unpleasantness of life and death on a daily basis, so, after a few detours in other careers, I became a writer (and deal only with imaginary traumas, except for my deadlines!). But I've always had a lot of animals in my household and can't imagine how lonely and unhappy life would be without them.

A special thanks to:

Rick and Pam Durst for the use of their beautiful house on Lake Travis. Your hospitality was warmly appreciated.

Jim and Barbara Williams for the delicious barbecue *and* the Bluebell Ice Cream. Boy, do I miss that in Colorado!

Mimi Dalton for being such a sweetheart.

And to my precious Holly. You added so much joy to my life. You are missed.

Kathy Clark

Cast of Characters

AT THE FLYING HORSE

Bubba Gibson	A good ole boy.
Mary Gibson	His long-suffering wife.
Manny Hernandez	Veterinarian for many of the Crystal Creek ranches.

AT THE DOUBLE C RANCH

John Travis (J.T.) McKinney	Rancher, owner of the Double C, his family's ranch. A man who knows his own mind.
Cynthia Page McKinney	J.T.'s wife. An ex-Bostonian bank executive learning to do things the Texas way.
Tyler McKinney	J.T.'s eldest son, a graduate of Rice University. Now he wants to grow grapes in his daddy's pasture.
Cal McKinney	J.T.'s second son, an irresistible and irrepressible rodeo cowboy.
Serena Davis	The boot maker who turned Cal's head.
Lynn McKinney	J.T.'s only daughter. She bucks the trend by raising Thoroughbreds in quarter horse country.
Hank Travis	J.T.'s ancient grandfather. Old Hank has seen and done it all.
Ruth Holden	Californian vintner, daughter of Dan Holden, J.T.'s old army buddy. Ruth is helping Tyler plan his vineyard—and his life.

AT THE HOLE IN THE WALL

Scott Harris	He's exchanged his pinstripes for chaps and a Stetson, to create his dream, the Hole in the Wall Dude Ranch.
Valerie Drayton	Scott's new wife and partner in the ranch.
Tracey Cotter	New manager of Cal McKinney's new venture.

CHAPTER ONE

MANNY HERNANDEZ SLIPPED the truck's transmission into third gear and depressed the accelerator as far as he dared in the treacherous conditions. He'd tried to wait out the storm but changed his mind and decided to brave the elements. If he wanted to reach his parents' house in Corpus Christi at a reasonable hour, he had to get moving.

He turned up the volume on his radio to drown out the pounding rain. Garth Brooks crooned the words "and the thunder rolls..." just as a wave of thunder vibrated across the Hill Country, and Manny smiled at the timing.

As he passed the Now Leaving Crystal Creek sign, he settled back against the seat with a deep sigh. It had been a hell of a week. Manny had helped bring several foals into the world, had nursed a rather unhappy bull back to life and had had to euthanatize an aging horse, something he hated doing. But for a small-town vet in ranch country, it was all part of the job.

He was looking forward to a well-deserved break from the grind, relaxing and enjoying all the non-stop food his mother would feed him. Because his culinary talents were limited, he'd really learned to appreciate her talents since he'd moved away from home.

The rain wasn't letting up. It sheeted down the windshield in a blinding torrent. Where was the warmth the weather forecaster predicted two days ago? Enough water had collected on the two-lane blacktop road to make hydroplaning a real threat, and Manny eased back on the accelerator and flipped the wiper blades on high.

At this speed, he realized the trip would take forever. And he had a real craving for green chili, the way only his mother knew how to make it.

He rounded a curve and peered through the gloom as his headlights caught a glint of something shimmery. This part of the state was famous for its abundant wildlife, so Manny moved his booted foot onto the brake pedal. Squinting through the blurred glass, he systematically scanned the terrain for deer.

After a few seconds, he realized what he'd seen was a car's headlights. But they weren't moving any closer.

He slowed, edging forward until he saw that a car towing a hopelessly jackknifed rental trailer had partially slid off the side of the road and was now stuck in the soft mud and gravel shoulder.

Obviously, the accident had just happened, which meant someone might be hurt or, at the very least, need help. Manny debated his options, his desire to make tracks toward his parents' warring with his strong instinct to save and heal.

His instinct won.

Turning on the truck's hazard lights, he pulled off the road behind the car, then reached for his black felt Stetson, which he'd casually tossed on the seat beside him. He dug under the seat for his emergency kit and grabbed a rain slicker, then took out a flashlight and fresh batteries. He'd learned the hard way always to be prepared. In his business—and his life—it had paid off...more than once.

Wind and rain buffeted him when he opened the truck door. He angled his Stetson, futilely trying to keep his face as dry as possible as he fought his way across the road to the front of the car.

A slim boy was kneeling on the ground, obviously with no regard for the wet or the cold as he stroked the neck of a deer he'd apparently hit. The rain had plastered the teenager's short dark hair against his head, and his thin cotton shirt stuck to his back. Even though the temperature was probably hovering around seventy, the cold rain had to be chilling the boy to the bone.

"Need some help?" he asked softly, so as not to frighten the deer—or the boy. The vet knew that both were likely in a state of shock.

The boy glanced over his shoulder, then stood. The beam from Manny's flashlight swept from the person's head, down a slender, but very feminine body to a pair of expensive-looking cowboy boots that were rapidly getting ruined. He lifted the light, angling it so it wasn't shining directly into the woman's eyes.

Drops of water glistened on her long dark eyelashes. His gaze was drawn to her eyes, large luminous eyes that held a flood of guilt as she lifted her hands in a helpless gesture. "I swerved to miss another deer... then this one darted in front of me. I tried to avoid him, but..." Her voice faded into a shudder.

"It wasn't your fault. Deer get hypnotized by the lights, then become too paralyzed to move."

"I think he's still a baby."

Manny knelt next to the deer, noticing she'd somehow managed to get the animal partially onto a blanket. "Well, actually she's a full-grown sika deer. They never lose their spots, so they're often mistaken for fawns."

"Do you think she's going to be all right?"

Manny heard the note of near panic in the woman's voice and was almost as worried about her as he was about the deer. "It's too early to tell. She needs immediate medical attention and a dry place to spend the night," he said honestly. As much as he wanted to give good news, it wasn't always possible. "Here, hold this flashlight for me."

She knelt next to him and focused the light where he indicated. Her free hand moved over the animal's long, graceful neck and slender head. He did a cursory check of the doe, all the time aware of the woman's shaking hands. "Is this your blanket?" he asked, more to keep her distracted than anything else.

"I've been trying to move her farther off the side of the road, but didn't have much luck."

"Good thinking. Let's see what we can do to save this little lady."

So much for a weekend of R and R.

Manny climbed into the cab, turned the engine on and swung the vehicle into a U-turn. He braked to a halt when the bed of the pickup was even with the terrified deer and the equally frightened woman.

The noise of the mechanical tailgate lift being lowered drowned out the sound of the rain for a few seconds. The deer's huge eyes stared up at the woman, as if seeking reassurance.

"It's okay, sweet thing," Manny said, again joining the two on the rain-soaked highway. "Just a few more minutes, and we'll be on our way."

FOR THE FIRST TIME since the horrible ordeal began, Tracey Cotter felt a tinge of genuine relief. When the first animal had run out, she'd reacted quickly and automatically, swerving to the opposite side of the road. But after only a few seconds of satisfaction that she'd managed to miss the animal, she'd felt a thud and heard a sickening crunch.

The safety belt had sliced into her stomach and shoulder. The steering wheel jerked from her hands when the tires hit the soft wet gravel on the side of the road. Though she'd struggled to bring the vehicle under control, the weight of the loaded trailer threw it off balance. The car skidded in one direction and the trailer went in another until it became mired in the ditch.

The car's single working headlight provided just enough visibility for her to see how awful her situation truly was. Through a curtain of steam rising from her dented hood, she searched the semidarkness. Finally, realizing she would have to get out into the raging storm sooner or later, she'd climbed out of the car.

Another deer, slightly smaller than the first, lay sprawled across the road. At first, Tracey thought it was dead, but as she stood, horrified, staring down at the once graceful body, the creature had lifted its head. Groggily, it had looked up at her, its dark eyes wide and frightened. It struggled to stand, but could do little more than move its neck and head. Pathetic bleating sounds emerged from its mouth, and Tracey tasted the salt of her tears as she bent down. She'd never felt more helpless in her life.

But then, just as in a movie, a tall handsome stranger had shown up and immediately taken control.

"Can you give me a hand?" the man asked. "As you've found out, just because she's small doesn't mean she's light."

Tracey nodded, flexing her aching muscles. After hauling all her belongings from an upstairs apartment and stacking them in the trailer earlier that morning, and then trying to move the deer single-handedly, she knew she'd pay the price tomorrow. And there was still the unloading to face. Fortunately, her friends Cal and Serena had agreed to come over and help. Unfortunately, it would be up another flight of stairs to a small apartment over a garage.

"While I pick her up, maneuver the blanket under her." The man's attention was focused on the animal as he stroked the short, spotted coat.

His words offered her no options. She balanced the flashlight on the bumper of her car so they could see between the blinding flashes of lightning. Then she crawled around to get a good grip on the edge of the square of woolen cloth.

Even with the two of them, it took several more minutes to get the animal onto the blanket. It didn't help that the doe kept floundering, desperate to escape into the security of the woods.

The night continued to grow colder, and Tracey began to wonder if she'd ever be warm again. She wasn't sure if the chattering of her teeth was caused by the weather or the shock of the accident. But she did notice that the man kept giving her worried looks.

"Okay, now we have to move her onto the lift," he said, once they had centered the deer on the cloth.

It was easier said than done. As they struggled, sweated and strained, Tracey decided that she would rather not deal with frightened wildlife again. The doe squirmed and fought, even though the man kept a tight grip on her fetlocks to keep her razor-sharp hooves from hurting either of them.

Finally, the man climbed into the bed of the truck and brought out a small leather halter and some rope.

"I was hoping I wouldn't have to do this, but I don't have anything to anesthetize her with until we get her to my place," he said to Tracey. Moving swiftly and smoothly, he slipped the halter over the animal's head and fastened a strap under her jaw. Then, after inching the blanket toward the cab, he unrolled the ropes and secured them at the four corners of the truck's bed. After making sure everything was secure and the animal couldn't move, he vaulted off the tailgate.

The Stetson didn't make it. It landed upside down on the ground, the edges of its curled brim brushing the mud.

Tracey picked up the hat and turned it over, letting the water that had collected in it drain out before she wiped it off as best she could. But her fingers were muddy, so she only made it worse.

He glanced at the Stetson, then fixed on Tracey's apologetic expression. A slow, sexy grin stretched across his full lips and added a twinkle to his eyes . . . eyes as dark as the moonless Texas night.

"Thanks," he said, his voice as low and gentle as when he'd spoken to the deer.

Suddenly very aware that she was on a deserted highway in the middle of a storm with her clothes plastered wetly to her body, Tracey thrust the hat toward him. As he reached out and accepted it, their fingers brushed and a sensation of awareness shivered up her spine.

"Good thing it's not a ten-gallon hat," she said, struggling to keep her tone light.

"A gallon's enough for me," he agreed.

"Are you going to take the deer to a vet?"

"Sort of."

She gave him a puzzled look.

"I'm taking him back to my place."

"Your place?"

"We haven't formally met." He swept the Stetson against his chest and bent in a courtly bow. A thick lock of damp black hair fell across his brow. "I'm Manuel Hernandez ... Manny," he told her. "I *am* Crystal Creek's vet."

He extended his hand and she took it. Her small fingers disappeared in his grasp, which was warm and intensely comforting.

"Well, Manuel—"

"Manny."

"Manny," she acknowledged. "I'm very pleased to meet you. And thanks for all your help."

"The pleasure's mine." He paused for a second. "Ma'am ... ?"

"Tracey," she supplied. "Tracey Cotter. My mother's the 'ma'am' in the family."

"Does she live in Crystal Creek?"

"No, my parents are still in Wolverton. That's where I grew up."

"I assume you were heading there...Crystal Creek, I mean."

"*Was* is the operative word." In spite of everything, she still remained partially optimistic. Serena had always said that optimism was Tracey's greatest asset and also her biggest downfall. But Tracey refused to let minor setbacks get her down. It couldn't be too much farther to the town. She would worry about the car tomorrow.

"Your car's in pretty bad shape," Manny commented, as if reading her mind.

She looked over at the vehicle. The remaining headlight had been growing steadily dimmer, testimony to the fact she'd probably drained the battery in addition to heaven-only-knew what else.

"Why don't I give you a lift into town?"

"That won't be necessary, Manny. Thanks anyway."

He looked first at the car, then back at her. Even in the minimal amount of light, she read skepticism in his gaze.

"Look, Tracey, it's obvious that this car isn't going anywhere tonight. Why don't I pull it out of the ditch in the morning when things have dried out and we'll find out what's wrong with it. Right now, we're both drenched and this animal needs attention right away. Besides, I could use your help. I'm sure I couldn't find my assistant at this time on a Friday night."

Put like that, there was no way she could refuse. "Okay. But will my things be okay here?"

"Who would be crazy enough to be out on a night like this?" Again, that sexy smile flashed white against the darkness of the night. A crack of lightning danced across the sky and was captured in the flirtatious twinkle in his eyes. "Let's go." He slammed the tailgate shut and fastened it securely.

Tracey sloshed back to her car, turned off the barely burning headlight, grabbed her purse, then locked up.

Even though the rain continued to pelt both of them, Manny walked with her to the passenger side of his vehicle, then held the door open for her. Tracey struggled to take the high first step, convinced the denim encasing her leg must have shrunk during the past hour. Her breath caught in her throat as Manny's big hands spanned her waist and lifted her onto the seat.

"Thanks," she managed to squeak out.

Manny didn't seem to notice her discomfort. Or, if he did, he was gentleman enough not to react. He walked around the front of the truck and slid behind the wheel, then turned the heater fan on high. As the warmth filled the cab, Tracey tried to relax.

"It's only a few miles," he assured her as they cut their way through the thick, stormy night.

"Where were you planning on staying?"

"I rented an apartment from Marguerita Sanchez."

"So you're the boot lady?"

She glanced at him in surprise.

"It's a small town," he offered in explanation. "Someone new moving here always causes a stir. And Serena was talking about you down at the Longhorn. You're partners?"

"News really does travel fast."

"So it's pretty accurate?"

"In this case."

"You'll be running the boot shop at the Hole in the Wall Dude Ranch?"

"That's the plan. I'm looking forward to the change of scenery." And change of people, she mentally added.

Her parents had been pressuring her to settle down and provide them with a grandchild to bounce on their knees. Conveniently, Donna Cotter had even chosen a prospective husband—a Baptist preacher's son who was considering the seminary himself. At every family gathering Tracey had attended for the past five months, Bryce had been present. Both sets of parents fawned over him and continually sang Tracey's praises to him.

And Donna had actually exaggerated a few of Tracey's virtues . . . like the fact that she was an excellent cook. That was more than an exaggeration. It was an out-and-out fib. Tracey was good in the kitchen . . . as long as the meal was in a ready-to-cook microwave container. Or soup. She heated a great can of soup.

According to her mother, by the age of twenty-six most women were married. But Tracey hadn't yet found anyone special. And she'd settle for nothing less than the kind of relationship Serena had found with Cal.

Tracey was genuinely glad for her friend, but she was human enough to admit to an occasional twinge of envy. Cal treated Serena like a princess. Tracey wanted that same kind of unconditional love in her life. But it wouldn't happen with Bryce. And the more her parents pushed, the more she rebelled.

Manny slowed the truck. "We're almost there."

Tracey glanced through the rear window to check on the deer and saw that the animal's eyes were open wide.

"She okay?" Manny asked.

"She's still scared."

He nodded. "We'll get her patched up soon."

"I really appreciate everything you've done."

"It's my job."

"Your approach seems to go beyond that," she commented.

He glanced at her. "What makes you say that?"

"When I was a kid I had a cat who dislocated his hip, and we had to take him to the vet."

"And?" Manny prompted when she trailed off.

"The vet was clinical, cold...as if he didn't care. He treated my cat as a job, not as a part of my family...which, of course, he was."

"Pets are a very important part of people's lives," he agreed. "But I specialize in large-animal care. Horses and such."

"So you're the perfect person to help Sweetie."

"Sweetie?"

"The deer."

"You named her?" he asked with evident surprise.

"You're the one who called her 'sweet thing.' I was trying to calm her down. She's so innocent and sweet...it just seemed natural."

His chuckle warmed her. No wonder animals reacted so well to his kind and gentle tone. It was doing strange things to her equilibrium, too.

Manny stopped, then backed the truck into the long driveway and used a remote control to open the huge barn door. "At least we won't have to get much wetter than we already are," he said, after turning off the engine.

"I'm afraid your seat is soaked."

He lifted one broad shoulder in a shrug. "It'll dry."

Working side by side, they managed to get Sweetie into the barn and settled in a cozy, clean stall. Manny hung his slicker on a peg and rolled up his sleeves. Tracey stood back and watched as he examined the frightened animal.

"Would you come over here and pet her?" he asked. "She seemed a lot calmer when you were talking to her."

Tracey did as he asked, glad to feel useful. His long, tapered fingers stroked and probed the velvety fur and she could see how skilled they were at healing.

"She doesn't seem as bad as I first thought," he said after a couple of minutes.

"Thank goodness."

"She's lucky. But she'll need time to recuperate and let her right leg rest. She's probably got a hairline fracture, or at the very least, a major sprain." He stood, headed to a large, glass-fronted cabinet and gathered some medical supplies.

Tracey looked away while he administered a sedative. But she listened as he continued to soothe Sweetie until the animal fell asleep. Again, his compassion stirred her.

She managed to swallow her discomfort as she watched him stitch the animal's wounds, then tape and splint her leg.

"I'll check on her several times through the night." He stood and offered his hand. "How about a cup of coffee and a chance to really dry off?"

Now the ordeal was nearly over, she noticed that her fingers were numb and her clothes were stuck to her skin. A bath, fresh clothes and something warm in her stomach sounded like heaven.

Unfortunately, she didn't have a car or keys to her apartment. It was getting a little late to call Señora Sanchez and she hated to impose on Serena at such short notice. "Does Crystal Creek have any hotels?"

"A couple of motels, but they're sure to be full. There's some sort of regional 4-H event going on."

She sighed.

"Come on, Tracey, you deserve a break after all you've been through."

His offer tempted her.

"Cream and sugar?" he added.

"Deal."

He grinned.

She smiled in return.

"We'll go out the side door. There's a covered walkway all the way to the back porch."

No more rain. What a blessing! Tracey thought. Manny fastened the stall, then led the way to the exit. He closed the barn door, sealing in the warm, comforting scents of leather and hay.

He took her elbow as he guided her toward the house. Once inside, he shut the door behind them, then turned on the light.

The kitchen was large and homey. Even though it had the usual assortment of cooking utensils, it seemed to Tracey to be somehow very masculine.

A quick glance around proved he was most likely a bachelor. An empty milk carton sat on the table. A cat dish stood empty near the refrigerator, and there was a half dozen cups and bowls and a variety of silverware in the sink.

"I need to use your telephone, if you don't mind."

"It's on the back wall over there," he said, pointing. He took off his Stetson, shook the water off, then hung the still dripping hat on a hook by the door before he raked his long fingers in wet trails through his thick black hair. "I'll put the coffee on."

"Sounds wonderful." Tracey located the phone and dialed her parents' number. As the ring echoed in her ear, she turned around, watching Manny preparing the coffee.

"Tracey!" her mother declared exuberantly. "I was getting worried, what with the time and the weather."

"Nothing to worry about, Mom. I'm in Crystal Creek, safe and sound." She became silent as her mother flooded her with questions. "No...no problems whatsoever."

Manny turned toward her, arching a dark brow in curiosity. She flushed at the lie and his frank appraisal of it. But Manny didn't know her mother, and certainly couldn't imagine how her parents would react at the news that she was standing in the kitchen of a man she hadn't met until an hour ago. "Sure, Mom, everything's fine. I'll give you a call tomorrow."

She hung up, feeling a huge sense of relief that she'd skated through without her mother suspecting she wasn't really at Señora Sanchez's home. "My mother would get hysterical if she knew about the accident," she said to Manny, feeling a need to explain, but not knowing why.

"Ah," he said, apparently not completely convinced it was as simple as that, but not willing to push the issue.

The coffee began to gurgle and drip into the pot.

"I need to make one more call," she said.

"Be my guest."

Tracey dialed Serena and wasn't surprised when Cal answered, greeting Tracey warmly. Serena picked up the extension, cheerful as always.

"Welcome to Crystal Creek!"

"I'm glad to be here."

"I was afraid you'd be delayed by the weather. I can't believe how nasty it is."

"Actually, the trip wasn't completely uneventful."

"Oh?"

Tracey and Serena knew each other far too well to try to hide their feelings. When Serena and Cal had gone through some difficult times, Tracey had clued in instantly, even when it was obvious Serena wished Tracey would mind her own business.

"I had an accident . . . hit a deer, actually."

"My God, are you all right?"

"Just shaken up. And cold."

"Do you need me to come over?"

"I'm not at the apartment." Tracey twisted the tight, snaking curls of the phone cord around her index finger. "The local vet stopped to help me."

"Manny?"

"You know him?"

"Everyone knows Manny," Serena said. "He's got quite a reputation with animals. With women, too."

Tracey caught a hint of a warning in Serena's tone. "I'm at his house right now. We just finished taking care of the deer. He thinks she's going to be okay."

"I see. So are you going on to your apartment tonight?"

"I imagine Manny could give me a lift. My car's still stranded at the side of the road."

"Do you want me to come and pick you up?" she offered once again.

Feeling Manny's gaze, Tracey turned.

"Trace?" Serena's voice vibrated across the wire.

"I'll make sure you get home," Manny said.

Tracey met his eyes across the room and her decision was quick and easy.

"No, thanks, Serena. Manny said he'd get me home."

After a few silent seconds, Serena finally said, "The move-in party is still on for ten tomorrow morning."

"Good." Tracey was relieved at the change of subject. "I'll definitely need the help. I didn't know I had so much stuff."

Serena laughed, albeit a little hollowly. "I know how that goes."

Both said their goodbyes, but before she could replace the receiver, she heard Serena call her name.

"Trace?"

"Yeah?"

"Manny's a great guy. But be careful."

Neither had to mention the incident in Tracey's past that still haunted her. But it was paramount in both their minds. "Don't worry, Serena. Everything's under control. Good night."

This time she truly did hang up.

"Don't tell me," Manny said, filling a cup for her and stirring in a spoon of sugar, "Serena told you all the details of my sordid past?"

"Are there many?"

He shrugged those incredibly strong, broad shoulders again. "Depends on what you'd consider too many."

She returned his grin. His words were almost too outrageous. Tracey walked a few steps across the floor to where he stood and accepted the extended cup. She tried not to notice the way several strands of his hair curled on his forehead or how the heat and passion of the Texas thunderstorm seemed to be fading into the distance outside, but still flashing in the depths of his eyes. "Actually, Serena said you were a great vet."

CHAPTER TWO

"You know, Tracey, there's something about you that's intrigued me since I first saw you."

"Oh?"

He took her chin in his fingers, then tilted her head back a little. Manny wasn't extremely tall—probably a couple of inches under six feet. Yet next to him she felt small, vulnerable.

"Your eyes," he murmured. "They're such an unusual color...sort of green and sort of gold."

"My eyes?" she echoed weakly. His fingers still retained the warmth from her coffee cup. "They're just light brown." She'd always considered her eyes her most unexceptional feature. Most beauties had green or blue eyes. Not plain light brown...like hers.

"Light brown?" Manny repeated. He shook his head. "Light brown doesn't begin to describe them."

She became aware of the texture of his fingers on her skin. His thumb rested in the cleft beneath her lips, the blunted end of his nail nearly brushing her lower lip. A feeling she'd long forgotten seemed to swirl to a life of its own.

"Amber," he said finally. "With spikes of pure gold."

"Gold?" She tried to suppress a smile, but couldn't. Tracey knew herself to be at least passably attractive, but the word most often used to describe her was "cute."

She briefly wondered if he might kiss her, and she realized, with a startled shiver, that she wanted him to.

But he didn't.

He released her and stepped away. *Get a grip, Cotter,* she told herself, pushing back a pang of regret. She'd known the man barely an hour. Serena would have been shocked to know Tracey had even entertained the idea.

Lately, Tracey hadn't dated much. She knew she shouldn't let what had happened color her relationships for the rest of her life, yet the memory still lurked. So she'd stuck to friendships with men, but nothing more serious.

"Would you like to take a quick shower?"

She shook her head. "No thanks. I'll just have the coffee. Then if you don't mind, you could give me a ride to Señora Sanchez's."

"You've got goose bumps all down your arms."

Despite the kitchen's warmth, she had to admit that she still felt chilled.

"And there's not a single dry spot on your jeans."

She glanced down. Manny was right. Her jeans were soaked. Every one of her curves was outlined in shrunken denim.

Her boots, hand-tooled only a week ago by Esteban at the shop in Wolverton, were ruined. Mud caked the sides and water had soaked into the leather. The mauve color was now mud-brown.

"Look, Tracey, I don't have any ulterior motives. I had a waterproof coat on and I'm cold. You go ahead and take a shower upstairs. I'll shower downstairs, then we'll meet back here in ten minutes and have a fresh cup of coffee."

"I don't know...."

"Suit yourself. But apparently Serena didn't tell you to hightail it out of here."

When she was going to protest, he held up a hand. "I'm not a saint, Tracey, and I'm not going to fool either you or myself. Serena probably told you to watch out, but I've never so much as kissed a woman who wasn't willing. I don't intend to start with you."

She wasn't sure whether to be relieved or disappointed.

"I'm going to take a shower and change out of these clothes. The guest bathroom's up those stairs, first door on the left. You'll find a robe and fresh towels. There should be soap and shampoo in the cupboard under the sink."

Without another word, he vanished. Tracey frowned. His suggestion went against everything her mother had taught her, and she knew she shouldn't accept his offer. And yet he'd been nothing but a perfect gentleman since she'd met him. The problem was, she realized, she was becoming more and more attracted to him.

Using his bathroom, his towels, his robe seemed too personal. And too tempting to resist.

From the next room, she heard him talking, probably on the telephone. The walls muted the richness of his voice, but she caught the occasional word of Spanish, then the brief goodbye, with a promise he'd call again soon.

Then she heard the sound of water running and thought of the warm vapor that would be surrounding him. Tracey moved to the window and saw huge raindrops splatter against the glass, then slide down to puddle on the ledge.

Another chill surged down her spine. Manny was definitely right about the goose bumps on her arms. And her skin had a bluish hue. She didn't need a cold or pneumonia to deal with when she was about to begin a challenging new business venture.

To get to the staircase, she passed through the living room and noted that it was just as homey as the kitchen. Photographs, some black and white, others color, each framed in wood, stood on oak end tables. A colorful afghan, knitted in the colors of the Mexican flag, was draped over the back of a large leather couch, and a rug, cinched in the middle, adorned the wall above the empty fireplace. Trophies marched across the mantel, and a sombrero hung haphazardly from a peg near the door. Manny's heritage was evident in the warm, welcoming room.

Tracey's boots echoed off the polished wood as she mounted the stairs. She found all the promised items in the bathroom, turned on the water and started unfastening the buttons on her still-damp flannel shirt.

It took a good deal longer to get out of the jeans. They fit tighter than a second skin. When she finally did shuck them, her legs were pale and had more goose bumps than her arms. A shower really *was* a good idea.

Before stepping into the warm spray, she noticed her reflection in the mirror, and groaned. Mascara, supposedly waterproof, was smudged around her eyes, raccoon fashion. Her hair hung in limp strands, and only a hint of lipstick gave any color to her face. Now she truly understood the meaning of the phrase "drowned rat."

No wonder Manny had said she was safe with him. The way she looked right now, she would have been safe with a man who had been all alone on a desert island for ten years!

She showered, savoring the difference between the warm water that now caressed her and the frigid rain that had drenched her earlier. The bar of soap, promising the freshness of spring, lathered in her hands and made her body slick with bubbles before they raced down the drain. She washed her hair and was rinsing it when she noticed the change in water pressure. Manny had probably turned his faucets off.

Manny.

Despite the way she'd looked, he'd said complimentary things about her eyes. And he'd been so kind about helping her with Sweetie. There was something about him, something *nice,* something that intrigued her. And something that warned her to keep well away.

By the time she'd dried herself with a large white towel, her optimism returned. Using the blow dryer, she brought her dark brown hair back to life. A thick fringe of bangs hung across her forehead, and the back was sculpted to a vee at her nape. With her fingers, she fluffed in body.

But still Tracey frowned at her reflection. Too bad she didn't have her cosmetics bag. She hadn't anticipated needing it until she went to work. Of course, she hadn't anticipated using the bathroom of a man she barely knew either.

She slipped into the robe hanging from the back of the door. It brushed her ankles, though she realized it was probably no more than knee-length on its owner. Faint traces of a very masculine, potent cologne reached her senses. A hot flush stole into her cheeks at the thought that the material hugging her naked body had touched Manny's in the same way.

So far, it had been a very memorable night.

Carrying her wet clothes, she descended to the kitchen. Manny stood near the coffeepot, cup in hand, looking out the window, toward the barn.

He turned.

She stood there, transfixed.

Without a doubt, he was one of the most attractive men she'd ever seen. His hair, dark as a Texas midnight, was parted on the side and brushed back from his face. Still, the errant strand she'd noticed earlier fell across his tanned forehead. His nose was slightly crooked, as if it had been broken in a long-ago fight, and his lower lip was full, sensuous. He hadn't shaved, and the shading of a heavy beard darkened his jaw. His red flannel shirt accentuated the richness of his deep skin tone.

But it was his eyes that riveted her attention, compelling her not to look away.

"More coffee?" he asked, as if she were an ordinary visitor, not a woman who'd just used his shower and his soap, and now stood in the middle of his kitchen floor, wearing nothing but his royal-blue robe.

"Thanks."

Manny nodded and filled her cup. "Here, let me throw these in the dryer for you," he offered, taking her soggy clothes.

While he was in the laundry room, Tracey knotted the belt tighter around her waist. Though he hadn't made any overtly sexual moves, her imagination was supplying plenty of its own.

What was getting into her? she wondered as she took a seat at the table.

Desperate for any explanation to justify her wayward thoughts, she told herself it must be the storm, the electricity in the air. Unbidden, her mother came to mind. Donna Cotter would be scandalized to know her only daughter was sitting at the table of a man she'd known for only a few hours.

"Looks interesting."

Tracey glanced up. Manny was back in the kitchen. "What does?"

"Whatever you're thinking. You're smiling."

He took the glass carafe from the burner, topped up both their cups, then sat across from her.

"I was thinking of my mother."

"Oh?"

"And wondering how long her swoon will last if she ever finds out I was here with you."

Manny grinned in sympathy. "You've got an interfering mother, too?"

"Too?"

"I get a call every Sunday morning, asking if I'd like to bring a lady companion to dinner. Every week for the past two years, she's gotten the same answer. But that doesn't stop her from calling at precisely eight a.m."

His chuckle was warm and husky, compelling her to join in.

Then just as suddenly, the atmosphere changed. He fixed her with his intensely dark eyes and appeared to want to say something, but instead he pushed back his chair.

"I'll go see how our patient's doing."

"Mind if I come?"

"Not at all." *Liar,* his conscience mocked. He wanted to escape to the barn to put some distance between him and Tracey.

As soon as he'd realized she was a woman, he'd begun to notice she had an unusual type of beauty. But it wasn't until she stood in his kitchen, bare toes with painted nails peeking out from beneath his too large robe, that longing hit him. And hit him hard. It had been a long time since he'd had a real relationship. "I think my mother left a pair of tennis shoes here the last time she visited. Let me see if I can find them."

He went into the living room, anxious to put some distance, however small, between them. He wondered if he wouldn't have been smarter taking her back to her car or on to her apartment the minute the injured animal had been settled. Just as quickly, he shoved aside the idea. Her car was obviously in bad shape, and at the very least was stuck in the mud. Trying to do anything to it in heavy darkness on nearly flooded roads wasn't smart.

He'd made the right decision.

Hadn't he?

He returned, carrying socks and the shoes that would probably be too large on her feet. He guessed she wanted to appear self-possessed and independent, but the truth was, there was something vulnerable about her that compelled him to want to protect and take care of her.

He held the door for her. Though the rain continued to beat on the roof and rush down the gutters, a scent of freshness lingered in the night. The storm was effectively marking the end of a late August heat wave that had baked the air and left the foliage wilted and brown. By tomorrow the grass would be a lush green.

Sweetie was asleep. Sweetie? When had he started thinking of the deer as Sweetie? Yet the fact that Tracey had named the injured animal endeared her to him. In his line of work he saw too often the results of neglect and mistreatment. Most people whose cars hit wildlife just continued on their way, not caring whether the animal lived or died.

He remembered the time he'd come across a wounded deer at the side of the road, in the middle of nowhere. He'd had no way to transport the animal, and no supplies to treat such serious injury. His examination showed that the animal wouldn't recover and was in great pain. Manny had been forced to euthanatize the animal. Without benefit of a gun.

Sweetie, though, had been luckier. It was impossible to be sure so soon, but he suspected she'd be all right and would someday return to the wild.

"Want to give me a hand?" he asked.

"Sure."

Together, they changed the bandages. Kneeling at the animal's side, he looked at his companion. Guilt was still reflected in her eyes. Her eyes. They were truly the most compelling he'd ever seen. A fascinating mixture of emerald and amber, they mirrored her thoughts. And he'd seen her run the gamut, from trepidation to uncertainty to guilt. And another emotion flickered in their depths, one he hesitated to name, because it would mean the spark he'd felt toward her was reciprocated.

"I tried not to hit her," she said softly. "She came out of nowhere...." Guilt dug its way even into her tone.

"It's not your fault, Tracey. Wild animals often behave unpredictably. Sometimes it's impossible to avoid a collision, even in the best weather."

"Thanks."

He noticed the way her small hands moved down the length of Sweetie's neck. Her motions were soothing, reassuring. For a few seconds, he thought of how those hands would feel on his skin... stroking, caressing, exciting...

"How much longer will it be?"

He blinked, startled back to reality. "Uh... how long will *what* be?"

"How much longer will she sleep?" Tracey restated her question.

"She'll be coming out of it soon. And I'm sure she won't be too happy to find herself locked in a barn."

"You know, when I was out there, in the middle of the highway, I prayed for help. I couldn't have asked for a better answer than you. You're obviously very good at your work."

Manny smiled. Healing was the thing he loved to do most, and to be appreciated for it just made it that much sweeter. "I do what I can," he commented modestly. "I'll check on her again in a little while."

They went back into the house.

"Shall I freshen your coffee?" she asked.

"Sure. It promises to be a long night."

Tracey looked at him, then returned the nearly empty pot to the burner.

"I like to keep my eye on patients that have suffered this kind of trauma." He held up a hand. "Wait, Tracey. I didn't say that to make you feel guilty. It's a fact of life, nothing more. You did wonderfully to stay with her and try to keep her calm. No one could ask for anything more.

"Look, it's late," he continued. "Why don't you just plan on spending the night? We can both get a fresh start in the morning."

"I appreciate the offer, but..."

"You've got a better suggestion?"

He watched her as she seemed to contemplate alternatives.

"No. But I should probably let Señora Sanchez know I won't be arriving till the morning."

"Give her a call. Then you can have one of the spare bedrooms upstairs. I'll sleep downstairs on the couch."

"That's not necessary, Manny. We're both adults."

That was what bothered him most. "It'll be easier for me to check on Sweetie."

"Thanks. I don't know how I'll repay your hospitality."

"No need. Actually, I spend more time on that couch than I do in my bed. I either accidentally fall asleep on it after a long, hard day, or I sleep on it because of the convenience. It's closer to the barn."

She smiled, and it seemed as if the sun had come out at midnight. "I didn't realize hospitality was a required class at veterinary school."

"No," he agreed easily. "It wasn't."

The dryer buzzed. "I'll get your clothes."

He returned a few minutes later, her blouse and jeans draped over his arm. "I think your shirt's the worse for wear."

She accepted the bundle. The now-faded shirt on top was a mass of wrinkles. "At least it's dry," she said.

"After what we've been through, that's a minor miracle."

Their eyes met yet again, and his breath caught in his throat. The effect this woman had on him was incredible.

"Good night," she said, breaking the charged silence first.

"Buenas noches," he replied. Although his mother and father had been born in Mexico, Manny was a native Texan. He spoke mainly English, but somehow good-night always slipped out in his parents' tongue.

She turned away from him. And he couldn't help noticing that even the baggy robe didn't hide the feminine swell of her buttocks.

At the door, she paused, then glanced over her shoulder. "I meant it when I said thanks for all you've done. You're a very special person."

"De nada," he said.

"I'll buy you breakfast at the Longhorn Coffee Shop," she offered. "Serena says they make the best breakfast in town."

"Nora brews a great cup of coffee, too."

The overhead light showed golden highlights in Tracey's hair that he hadn't noticed earlier.

"Then it's a deal?"

"Yeah, Tracey, it's a deal."

They both paused, their gazes still locked for a long, silent moment.

"Good night," she said, her voice barely more than a whisper.

After her quick phone call, he watched her climb the stairs and didn't turn away until he saw a shadow in the hallway after the bathroom door closed and the light was turned on.

Outside the living room window, a flash of now-distant lightning brightened the night, and a corresponding jolt of electricity made his skin tingle. Yes, Garth had hit it right on the money with that song, Manny thought. When the lightning struck, it struck hard and unexpectedly.

THE SCENT OF COFFEE brought Tracey instantly awake.

Usually, she stayed in bed, refusing to admit it was time to wake up until the last possible moment. But this morning was different.

Tracey sat up, her heart pounding. Nothing looked familiar. She rubbed her eyes, and blinked several times in rapid succession. Then she remembered.

Manny's house.

Sunlight filtered through the drapes, proving the rain had stopped sometime during the night. She glanced around the room she'd been too tired to notice the previous night.

Like the rest of the house, the walls were the original, decorator-inspired off-white. Pictures with a Southwestern theme hung on the walls. She wondered if Manny had chosen them himself, or if someone else had.

If so, who?

She heard sounds from downstairs and searched around for a clock. Not seeing one, she reached for the robe, wrapped it around her and slid her arms into the oversize sleeves before getting out of bed. Then, after stopping in the bathroom, she headed for the kitchen.

Pausing in the doorway, she studied the man bent over the newspaper, mug of coffee not far away. This morning he wore a black turtleneck. He'd obviously just showered, for his hair lay in schooled lines and the ends were still damp. She wondered if the errant lock would work its way down once it dried?

Sensing her presence, he looked up and greeted her with a friendly smile.

She smiled back.

"Morning," he said. "I wondered what it would take to get you out of bed."

"The coffee," she admitted.

"It's the second pot."

Guiltily, she looked at the digital clock on the microwave. "I had no idea it was that late."

"Don't worry. After last night, you obviously needed the rest. It's a good thing they serve breakfast all day at the Longhorn, though."

His grin was infectious. Too bad he wasn't a people doctor, she mused. His bedside manner would have been sensational.

"Serena already called. She figured she'd try here when she couldn't locate you at Señora Sanchez's. I made arrangements for her to meet you at your apartment about an hour later than planned."

Somehow, Tracey didn't mind his interference. In fact, she welcomed it. "When did she call?"

"Forty-five minutes ago."

"I can't believe I didn't even hear the phone."

"Like I said, you must have needed the sleep."

Without asking, Manny poured her a cup of coffee. He motioned her to a seat, added the right amount of sugar and cream, then placed the steaming brew in her hands.

"How's Sweetie?"

"Anxious to be up and about."

"But?"

"But her leg won't cooperate. What we have in the barn is one frustrated deer."

"Just like you predicted. Mind if I go see her before we leave?"

"Sure. I'll check her bandages again."

Tracey enjoyed the coffee. And the company. He entertained her with tales of Crystal Creek and filled her in on some of the more colorful local characters. From Serena, she'd heard many of the same stories, but Manny managed to give them a fresh appeal and a whole new perspective. It seemed that right now the talk of the town was her own imminent arrival. Last week it had been the fact that Jeff Harris and Hank Travis's oil well had come in and that it was a real gusher. Since Jeff's girlfriend, Beverly, was Cal's cousin, Tracey had already heard from Serena of Jeff's uncanny knack for finding oil. And she'd heard all about what an unusual couple Beverly and Jeff made. So she knew that, in a few days, new gossip would replace the story of her move to the small town.

When she felt human again, Tracey excused herself to get dressed. The jeans looked okay, but the shirt certainly didn't. She began to regret her impulsive invitation to breakfast.

Oh well, she decided, last night she'd looked like a drowned rat, and this morning she was more like the "something" the cat had dragged in. She smoothed the wrinkles as best as she could before meeting Manny in the kitchen again. "Have you seen my boots? I thought I left them in the bathroom last night."

"You did. They're near the back door."

She crossed to where he indicated. "Manny, you didn't need to clean them," she said, touched that he'd thought of it. They'd never be good for anything except farm work, but optimistically, she realized it was a small price to pay considering all that had happened the previous night.

He shrugged.

"It seems I'm even further in your debt."

"I wouldn't worry about it," he said. "I couldn't have saved your deer by myself."

He led the way to the barn. Tracey's heart went out to Sweetie. The animal was on her feet, but she was struggling to stay balanced on her three good legs.

"Hi, my pretty girl," Tracey murmured. "It looks like you're going to make it. You sure had me worried last night."

Manny was leaning against a post, studying her intently.

"You have a knack with animals."

"I've always loved them, especially deer. I still cry at *Bambi*."

"You're a soft touch."

"And you're such a tough guy," she said, then grinned. "Which is why you were petting her and crooning to her last night."

"Crooning?" he echoed. "I did no such thing."

"You did."

"I did?"

"You did."

He laughed, and she enjoyed the intoxicating sound of it.

For a few more minutes, she petted Sweetie, promising her that she was in good hands. But Tracey suspected the deer already knew that, because she showed no sign of fear whenever Manny stepped closer. "How long do you think you'll have to keep her?"

"I'm not sure. It can take a while for sprains to heal, and I wouldn't feel comfortable releasing her until she's capable of fending for herself again."

"I'd like to see her again."

"I'd like that, too."

Suddenly, she realized they weren't talking about Sweetie. But neither she nor Manny was ready to explore any more personal possibilities at the moment.

"Come on, Tracey Cotter, I'm starving," Manny said, his tone light. But his eyes were dark and sensuous.

She was able to hide the sudden rush of color to her cheeks as she told the deer goodbye. Manny held the door open for her and she hurried past him.

Outside, the air smelled fresh and clean. Not a single cloud marred the blazing blue of the sky.

Except for the huge puddles of muddy water, not a trace of last night's storm remained.

Manny helped her into the pickup, his hand lingering longer than necessary on her arm. But she didn't object. Easily, he was the most handsome man she'd ever met. Certainly, he was the most gorgeous guy she'd been to breakfast with.

It figured she'd have no makeup and no fresh clothes. Timing was everything, and Tracey's was always just a little bit off the mark.

CHAPTER THREE

"SO YOU'RE THE GAL who works with Serena," Bubba Gibson said.

Tracey nodded. She glanced over at Manny, who was waiting patiently. He'd been greeted warmly by everyone they'd passed in the Longhorn, and he was taking the time to stop at every table to introduce her to the citizens of Crystal Creek.

"Seen some of the stuff she does," Bubba continued. "Looks good to me. Hell, I've even been thinkin' of gettin' me a pair of those fancy duds. Anyway, I heard folks are real happy about the new *boot*-ique at the Hole in the Wall."

She forced herself to smile at his pun. "Thanks for the encouraging words. I'm very excited to be here."

"Say, Doc, there's a horse I've been thinking about buying over in Austin. Quite a deal." He whistled softly. "You wouldn't have time to take a look at the little filly sometime this week, would ya?"

"Sure, Bubba. Give me a call."

"I'd appreciate that. I'm anxious to get going on my new business."

"A new business, Bubba?"

"Yep. Gonna start racin' me some horses."

Tracey noted the beaming look on Bubba's face, as well as the surprised expression on Manny's.

"Horse racing?" Manny asked.

"Just all kinds of money out there, waiting for me to come and get it. I aim to do just that."

"Well, I wish you luck. Horse racing isn't exactly a secure business."

"Ain't gonna be luck, Manny. No, sirree. It's gonna be skill." He rubbed his hands together. "Yep, this time I got it all figured out right. I'm gonna run it like a businessman would. That's why I'm needin' your help."

"Happy to oblige," Manny responded.

They said goodbye to Bubba and the female friend he hadn't introduced, and continued toward a booth in the back of the restaurant.

Red-and-white checked oilcloth draped the tables and a melancholy tune drifted from one of the old-fashioned jukeboxes. In fact, "old-fashioned" was the term Tracey thought best described the whole town. The buildings were neat and well maintained, but they had the dignified solidity of older construction. The people were casual, comfortable with the familiarity of folks who had either grown up together or who had a lot in common. Even the atmosphere was slower and gentler, as if time had stood still and the frantic 90's hadn't quite made it past that Crystal Creek city limits sign.

A waitress hustled over, a pot of coffee in hand. "Mornin', Manny."

"How's that calf doing, Margie?"

She smiled widely. "Like there was never a problem. You're a miracle worker. A real miracle worker. This time last week, we didn't think she was going to make it, but now she's up and bounding around the pasture. I've been telling everyone about it."

Margie, the wife of one of the hands at the Circle T, poured the coffee, then took their orders without ever offering a menu. But Manny obviously didn't need one.

"Come here often?" Tracey teased.

Manny smiled, then said, "I don't like to cook."

They talked about their food preferences and the advantages of modern conveniences until their meals arrived.

"Surprised to see you this morning, Manny. Thought you said you were heading to Corpus for the weekend," Margie commented.

Manny liberally sprinkled Tabasco sauce on his eggs, but gave the waitress his entire attention. "I was heading that direction, but I had a change of plans."

After the waitress left, Tracey set down her cup and frowned. "I'm sorry, Manny. I didn't mean to interfere with your plans to go to Corpus Christi. You shouldn't have stopped."

"No harm done," Manny said. "I was going to spend the weekend with my parents, but they understand medical emergencies always take precedence. It's one of the hazards of the job."

So that was who he'd called the night before. She felt an inexplicable sense of relief.

After breakfast, he paid the bill, over her protests, and ushered her out the door.

"Let's go check out your car and see how much damage we're dealing with."

In the truck, he changed the country tape for one of a Spanish folksinger. "You don't mind, do you?"

"Not at all."

He looked over at her, evidently shocked when she started singing along, albeit off key. "Esteban—one of the employees back in Wolverton—has the same tape," she explained. "He plays it all the time. Grows on you after a while."

"You're full of surprises, Tracey." His teeth flashed whitely against the golden-bronze tone of his skin.

All too soon, they reached her car and the trailer. In the light, it looked bad, but not as bad as last night. One of the headlights was shattered, the grill bent, and, to add insult to injury, the friendly highway patrol had left her a welcome notice in the form of a ticket under one of the wiper blades.

She looked around for the deer she'd seen watching her last night, but there was no sign of them.

"Do you want to try it?" he asked.

Tracey unlocked the car door and got in. Not surprisingly, it refused to start.

"Let me get the cables and jump the battery."

Within minutes, the engine sputtered to life, coughing and choking in protest to last night's abandonment.

Manny instructed her how to get the trailer and car both going the same way, but she had the annoying tendency to turn the wheel in the wrong direction. As frustrating as the situation was, she had to admit to being grateful for Manny's help. He finally told her to scoot over, and he performed the task himself.

When the car was back on the road again, she let out a relieved sigh. Manny got out, his Stetson tipped to partially shade his eyes. He leaned down and looked at her through the open window, bracing his forearms on the door. "I'll follow you to Señora Sanchez's house."

"That's really not necessary, Manny. You've done a lot already," she protested. But to be truthful, she'd enjoyed her time with him and hated to see it end. "If you left right now, you would still have time to make it to Corpus."

"There'll be other weekends." He dismissed the importance of the visit with a shrug. "Besides, I need to stick around and keep an eye on your deer. But I might as well make sure you get into town without any more problems."

"Okay, you win." She raised her hands from the steering wheel in mock surrender. "Lead, I'll follow."

The grin that brightened those ebony eyes made her almost regret she'd agreed to spend some more time with him. She had a sneaking suspicion it wouldn't be enough. Not nearly enough.

He raised his hand to the brim of his hat and tipped it slightly. "The pleasure's all mine, ma'am." The tone held a hint of Southern drawl and Spanish flair, rolled into a sexy as sin conbination.

They merged with traffic and Tracey turned on the radio, tuning in to the station with the least static.

". . . It's ten-o-two on a gorgeous morning in Claro County. Local Crystal Creek temperature is

sixty-seven degrees, heading for a high in the low
eighties, under clear skies. The thunder and lightning are long gone and there's plenty of sunshine on
tap for the rest of your weekend. In the meantime,
we invite you to sit back, relax and enjoy a morning the way only Texas can provide. To help you
along, we'll start you off with a triple play of
smooth, easy-listening tunes from George
Strait...."

As the country star sang about relationships,
Tracey couldn't help wondering about her previous night's savior. She knew him to be handsome,
intelligent, well respected and compassionate. But
what else hid behind those intensely dark eyes?

She certainly didn't have time for any serious
thoughts about a relationship with a man. On
Monday, she was expected to start work. In the
meantime, she needed to get moved in, have a
meeting with Serena to discuss business, tour the
new boot shop and make sure everything was in
order.

Manny turned on the truck's signal light, then
eased the pickup to the side of the road. She followed, stopping the car and trailer in front of the
house number she'd memorized.

They both climbed out of their vehicles and stood
awkwardly on the curb. "Safe and sound, as
promised," he said, propping a foot on the dam-

aged front bumper. Even though his words were casual, he appeared as reluctant as she to end their time together.

Before either could say anything more, a woman in her late fifties hurried outside.

"Señora Sanchez," Manny said unnecessarily.

Tracey offered a warm smile. "Señora Sanchez, I'm Tracey Cotter."

"*¡Dios!* I was worried until you called last night."

"As I told you, I ran into some trouble on the way here."

"Manny, he help you, no? He's a good boy, that one."

He inclined his head, modestly accepting the compliment.

"Come in, come in, already. Both of you. I get you something cold to drink."

Tracey and Manny exchanged helpless looks. Even if they combined their efforts, they wouldn't have the force of personality to refuse Señora Sanchez's hospitality. Tracey suspected a level-five Gulf hurricane couldn't stand up to the older woman.

They followed her inside the small but comfortable home. Their hostess bustled about, filling glasses with ice and cold tea. Manny took a seat and spread his long, denim-encased legs in front of him, heels resting on the faded linoleum floor.

Tracey looked away, trying to focus her attention on something less distracting.

"My husband, he went to help judge the 4-H show." Señora Sanchez shrugged. "I'm sorry he's not here to help you move in. He was here earlier this morning. Maybe if you want to wait until tonight—"

"Not to worry, *Señora*, I have friends arriving soon."

"Good. And maybe Manny can—"

"No," Tracey said instantly, then looked between Señora Sanchez and Manny. The older woman looked confused, and unfortunately, Manny looked hurt. "That is, Manny has already done so much, I couldn't possibly ask—"

"You wouldn't need to ask, Tracey. I'm volunteering."

"Really, Manny, I've been too much trouble to you already."

"We've already determined that I don't have anything else to do this weekend. And there's nothing I like more than helping damsels in distress."

"In that case, how can I resist?"

"You can't. I hope."

Just then a car's honk signaled the arrival of Cal and Serena, and Tracey hustled outside to greet her friends. Señora Sanchez poured iced tea for everyone, then left them to themselves.

Serena wrapped Tracey in a big friendly hug, as did Cal. Cal and Manny exchanged handshakes, though Tracey detected a slight tension between the two men.

Obviously, Serena had some reservations about the night Tracey had spent at Manny's house. Tracey couldn't fault her friend for caring, though. She and Serena were close and had gone through a lot together as they'd struggled to make their business a success.

"Looks like you got everything here in one piece," Cal said. "But I think the car's going to be spending some time in the garage. I can get someone to take it in, Trace."

"Great. I'll be needing it next week, most likely."

Manny and Cal went to the trailer, while Tracey and Serena finished their iced tea.

"So?" Serena prompted.

"So what?" Tracey asked.

Serena sighed. "Don't be dense. How'd it go last night?"

"If you're asking if Manny was a gentleman, the answer's yes. A perfect gentleman. We didn't even sleep in the same room. Anything else for the grand inquisition?"

"I didn't mean it that way," Serena said, her tone defensive.

"I know, and I didn't take it that way. I know you're concerned, but I can take care of myself."

"It's not you I'm worried about. It's Manny. I haven't met a woman yet who didn't get swept away by that irresistible Latin charm."

"*You* didn't."

"Well . . . okay, I'm one, but—"

"And I'm another," Tracey declared. "Come on, Serena. You know I'm always cautious, especially where men are concerned."

"Hey, Trace! What the heck do you have in here, weights?" Cal demanded, struggling in the door with a heavy box.

Manny put down the stereo he was carrying and moved over to help Cal.

"Yep. The bench is in there somewhere, too."

"You're serious? These are actually weights?"

"'Fraid so."

Everyone pitched in with the unloading. At last, after helping with the couch and bed, Serena collapsed on a kitchen chair. "That's it. I'm exhausted. If someone doesn't feed me, and soon, I'll never help again."

"Tell you what," Tracey said, "let's have a late lunch as a housewarming party, just the four of us. That is, if you don't mind, Manny." It had been easy to automatically include him, and now she found herself practically holding her breath, waiting for his answer.

"Sure," he said with only the slightest hesitation.

"Wait a minute," Serena protested hurriedly. "I didn't mean you should cook."

"Thanks a lot," Tracey said. "I wouldn't poison anyone...."

"Wouldn't count on that," Cal interrupted good-naturedly.

Tracey glared, and continued, "Actually I was thinking that maybe we could get some take-out or something."

They all jumped as Manny's beeper sent out a shrill noise. "Sorry," he said, unclipping the pager and checking the numeric display. "If you'll excuse me a minute, I'll see if I can use Señora Sanchez's phone."

While Manny was gone, Tracey made some instant iced tea for her company, hoping she could manage at least that much without Serena wrinkling her nose.

Manny returned a few minutes later, apologetic. "I hate to run out on you, but Bubba is interested in a horse and he wants me to look at it, in Austin. Guess the opportunity came up sooner than he expected. Anyway, he wants my opinion." He turned to Tracey. "I'll have to take a rain check on lunch."

"How about dinner?" she offered impulsively. "All of you. I appreciate your help and would like to thank you personally." She glanced at Serena. "We could go out."

"Cal and I can't," Serena replied apologetically, but then brightened. "There's a small get-together over at the Double C this evening."

"Maybe another time, then."

"Actually, I was thinking maybe you and Manny could join us," Serena continued.

"That would be great," Cal confirmed. "The caterer always allows for a few extra."

"What do you say, Tracey?" Serena asked. "Say you'll come. It'll be a good way for you to meet people who can steer customers our way. I can't believe I didn't think of it earlier."

"In that case, count me in." Tracey pushed her bangs off her forehead and tried not to think about how much she would have to do to make herself look presentable by tonight.

"I'll pick you up," Manny volunteered.

Trying to ignore the surge of excitement that leaped within her at the prospect of spending another evening with Manny, Tracey nodded. After all, considering her car wasn't working properly and she didn't have a clue how to get to Cal's dad's ranch, Manny's offer was the friendly thing to do.

Tracey already knew that Manny had the makings of a good friend. But a wild tingle raced through her at the added thought that he'd make a wonderful lover, too.

"SHE LOOKS FINE, Bubba. She's got all the qualities to make a good racehorse and eventually a brood mare."

Bubba grinned.

"But are you sure you want to do this?" Manny ran his hands over the quarter horse's flanks. No doubt, she was a beautiful animal. But there were never any guarantees with racehorses. It wasn't just good conformation and bloodlines that made a winner. A horse had to have a special, indefinable quality that would drive it from the post to the finish line with an unquenchable desire to get there first.

All the way from Bubba's ranch to Austin, he'd spoken of nothing else but the horse, Flying Wind. He'd said it was fate, getting into the quarter horse racing business with a horse that had the same first name as his ranch, the Flying Horse.

Manny didn't believe in omens. Particularly with such a flimsy base.

"She's one mighty fine filly," Lester Cain, the owner, said.

"I'm not questioning that," Manny said, retaining a professional disinterest. In his years of practice, he'd learned that once a person made up his mind about an animal, there was little, if anything, Manny could say or do to change that feeling as long as the animal was healthy.

"And at that price, she's a bargain that ain't likely to come along again anytime soon."

"I'm not so sure about that."

The old man spit a stream of dirty, brown tobacco from the middle of his mouth. It landed only inches from Manny's toes. "Are you saying mah lovely little filly ain't worth nothin'? That she ain't a gr-reat bargain?"

"No, sir," Manny said patiently. "I'm just suggesting Mr. Gibson may be able to find a similar or better deal on another horse."

"But he wants this un here."

"Yeah, ain't she a beauty?" Bubba added with an enthusiasm that made it clear the deal was all but clinched.

Manny shook his head. "I can't stop you," he said, addressing Bubba. "But you're paying me for my expertise. If it was me, I'd shop around some more. It's never a good idea to buy the first horse you look at."

"But what about your professional opinion, Manny? Is there any reason she won't be good stock?"

"She's very healthy," Manny admitted reluctantly, knowing the answer would be taken out of context.

"She's a pur-fect little lady." Lester's sly grin confirmed he was already counting on the sale.

Manny said nothing. At this point, it was up to Bubba.

"If'n y'all don't take mah excellent deal, I got another interested party. Yessir, got someone else comin' by in a little while." The old man glanced at his expensive gold wristwatch. "Fact, they should be here any minute. Nice couple from Houston. Makin' the drive just to see this filly."

Something about the situation felt wrong to Manny. He knew enough about quarter horses and the state of Texas's economy to realize the price was ten thousand dollars too high, maybe even fifteen thousand.

But if Bubba's mind was set . . .

"How much did you say, again?" Bubba asked.

Manny rolled his eyes, then excused himself. He waited outside, foot propped on the bumper of Bubba's truck. A trailer was attached to the hitch. ". . . Just in case," Bubba had said. That, in itself, had spoken volumes about Bubba's intentions. He wanted this particular animal and had planned all along to buy her.

Manny wondered why the hell Bubba had even wasted his time?

After another twenty minutes of negotiation, Bubba emerged from the barn. "Well, Manny, looks like we got ourselves a deal. We're in business." He waved a piece of paper in the late-afternoon sun.

"Congratulations." Manny saw his hint of sarcasm go unnoticed.

"I've got to write him a check, then we'll load up my little lady." Bubba slapped Manny on the back, and then began to follow Lester back to the house. "Yessir, I do believe I've got me the beginnings of a new dynasty, if I may say so myself."

"You may," Lester agreed, producing a cigar and clamping it, unlit, between his teeth. Pulling Bubba aside, he said quietly, "I've got the name and phone number in my office of that fella you were asking about. Why don't we finish our business in there?"

The two men went into the house while Manny stayed behind. As he waited in the peaceful September afternoon, he let his thoughts wander back to the woman he'd met last night. Tracey Cotter was different from most of the women he'd dated. Usually, he was drawn to strikingly attractive females with long, voluminous hair and flirtatious glances. With her pixie haircut and her easygoing and completely natural charm, Tracey was incredibly easy to be with, probably his first-ever female friend. And the first woman who'd ever spent the night without sleeping with him.

Yes, Tracey was different. And he felt different when he was with her.

Bubba, his chest puffed out, swaggered to the truck. "Yes sir. My ticket to financial security has just been signed." He slapped Manny on the back again. "Well, son, let's get going. My future's awaiting."

CHAPTER FOUR

"A SMALL GET-TOGETHER" was the understatement of the year. By the time Tracey and Manny arrived at the Double C Ranch at eight o'clock, the driveway was filled with Cadillacs, Corvettes, pickup trucks and all manner of other vehicles.

Serena's descriptions of the place, though wonderfully entertaining, didn't do justice to the huge, sprawling ranch. Tracey felt as if she'd just been driven onto the set of "Dallas."

Serena hurried over to the pickup only seconds after Manny had hopped out and opened Tracey's door.

"I'm so glad you came!" Serena's long black hair fell in a straight shining curtain around her shoulders and her green eyes glowed with excitement.

"I thought you said this was going to be a small get-together," Tracey accused.

"Honey, this is small."

"By Texas standards," Cal said, joining them and slipping an arm around Serena's slim waist.

For a second, Tracey felt a twinge of envy for their happiness. Not that she was jealous... Serena deserved happiness more than anyone Tracey knew. Yet she wondered what it might be like to experience the same kind of unconditional love.

"There won't even be a hundred people," Serena commented. "Not unless everyone shows up."

Tracey groaned. A hundred people. Maybe she could sit in a corner by herself.

Or with Manny.

That thought cheered her immeasurably.

"I don't deal wonderfully with crowds," Tracey reminded her friend.

"This isn't a crowd," Serena insisted. "Just family and a few friends."

Twenty minutes later, Tracey had a splitting headache. Somehow, she'd become separated from Serena *and* Manny. She'd met so many people and pasted on so many false smiles that she thought her lips were glued to her teeth.

So much for sitting in a corner. She hadn't been left alone for five seconds, not to mention had the time to sit down. As soon as she spotted a vacant chair, she collapsed on it. Luckily, it was at the edge of the mob and even shaded by a rainbow-striped umbrella.

"Well, if it isn't the boot lady again."

She glanced up. "Bubba Gibson, right?"

He straightened the oversize silver belt buckle that nestled under a hefty potbelly. "I'm impressed you remembered."

"So am I," she admitted honestly. She wasn't usually good with names, but Bubba had made quite an impression.

"Mind if we join you and set a spell?"

"Please do," Tracey said, hoping her disappointment at losing her moment of privacy didn't show. "It's too hot for me."

"Yep, every time I think fall is coming, summer surprises us again."

Bubba dragged over two chairs, then plopped down on one and left the other for his companion, a gracious-looking woman.

"This is my wife, Mary," Bubba supplied.

"I'm glad to meet you."

Mary smiled, a soft, shy smile. When she spoke, it was with the same gentleness. "The pleasure is mine, I'm sure. Al mentioned he met you this morning."

Bubba stared at Tracey as if daring her to say anything about the woman he'd breakfasted with that morning at the Longhorn Coffee Shop. Tracey didn't. Mary seemed to be a sweet person, one Tracey wouldn't want to hurt.

"Got me a new quarter horse this afternoon. First of many more."

"Yes, Manny told me about it. Congratulations." She looked at Mary and said, "So you're getting into a new business."

"My husband is." If possible, Mary's voice was even quieter.

Tracey noticed some color had drained from Mary's face.

Bubba patted Mary's arm. "It'll be all right, honey. We ain't gonna go wrong with this. Trust me."

"I do, Al."

His chest seemed to swell.

Serena joined them, drink in hand. "Manny got held up talking Thoroughbreds with Lynn. Said to tell you he'd find you in a few minutes. Did you get an opportunity to look around?"

"In my spare time," Tracey responded.

"Oh, stop." Serena squeezed Tracey's arm. "J. T. McKinney knows how to throw a do. Even a small one."

"I'll say."

"Cal's grandfather is anxious to meet you," Serena told her. "And he doesn't like to be kept waiting."

"A pleasure to have met you," Tracey said to Mary.

"Likewise. I'm sure you'll grow to love Crystal Creek."

Tracey stood and followed Serena.

"Cal's grandfather, Hank, is quite a character," her friend warned, while leading Tracey toward the shade of a huge oak tree. "He's ninety-nine and determined to hang in there at least until his hundredth birthday. With his temperament, he'll make it, too. He's giving George Burns a run for his money."

Before they reached Hank, the most striking woman Tracey had ever seen stopped Serena.

"So this is your partner. Welcome to Crystal Creek, Tracey. I'm Beverly Townsend. I was hoping to have the opportunity to meet you." The beautiful blonde held out a slender hand and greeted Tracey with a huge, sunny smile.

"Thanks," Tracey said, not really needing the introduction. From Serena's description, she would have known Beverly anywhere. She'd expected the beauty, but not the warmth, and Tracey was looking forward to getting to know the former beauty queen better.

Tracey had never been part of anything like this gathering before. The guests all seemed members of a huge, tightly-knit family. "Everyone has made me feel so welcome, so much a part of this community." She suspected it didn't hurt that she was Serena and Cal's partner in La Herencia Boot Stores.

"Well, we're delighted you're here," Beverly said sincerely. "I've heard so much about you from Serena. She says you're really good at what you do."

"I think we make a good team."

"We do," Serena asserted.

"I've been meaning to stop by and order a new pair of boots. Mine are positively wretched. When is convenient for you?"

"Any time," Tracey said. "Serena just introduced a few new designs, but we'd be just as happy to custom-design something for you."

"That's great. I'll pop in next week. Oh, if you'll excuse me, my mother has just arrived." To Serena, she said, "Go rescue your soon-to-be great-grandfather from Jeff, will you? Since the well came in, they've each been positively unbearable. And when you get them together..." Expressively, she rolled her eyes. But the smile on Beverly's face betrayed her words. She was obviously devoted to both men.

"Is she for real?" Tracey asked when Beverly drifted off. She followed the blonde's departure with admiration. She moved with a grace and poise Tracey could never hope to emulate.

"The ex-Miss Texas? Oh, yes, she's for real. I used to wonder the same thing, but everyone knows about her goodheartedness, and her charity work. Beverly's one of the most genuinely nice people you could hope to meet. When I first visited Crystal Creek with Cal and didn't know anyone, Bev made me feel right at home.''

They continued toward the tree where an older man, a blanket spread across his lap, and a younger man, obviously Jeff, Beverly's boyfriend, sat.

''Serena, glad to see you.''

Jeff stood, but Tracey felt the heat of the old man's gaze on her. Uncomfortably, she shifted.

Serena performed all the introductions. Tracey thought if she had to remember one more name, her brain would just disintegrate. But it wasn't difficult to mentally pair Beverly and Jeff. He was as handsome as she was beautiful. A perfect couple. More than ever, Tracy was aware of being alone.

''So you're the one everyone's been talkin' about,'' Hank said in what she gathered was his usual forthright manner.

''I could use a glass of punch. How 'bout you, Hank?'' Jeff asked, his gaze automatically fastening on Beverly as she talked to her mother.

''Don't need no punch unless it's spiked.''

Jeff and Hank exchanged sly winks, communicating in a silent code before the younger man left. Obviously, they'd done this kind of thing before.

Tracey detected a hint of a twinkle in the ancient eyes, as if he wanted to see just how much he could get away with. Tracey suspected it was a lot.

"You know what the doctor said," Serena reminded him, more because it was part of the game than because she was concerned.

"That young fool? He ain't even half my age."

Serena smiled tolerantly and turned to her friend. "Do you want some punch, Tracey?"

"Sure." Tracey slid a companionable glance at Hank. "I'll take what he's having."

Hank looked at Tracey, then nodded. "Smart girl. I like you. Now, come sit beside me. Keep an old man company for a few minutes."

She complied, stretching out her legs on the cool grass. Finally, she'd found a spot to relax where she could watch the crowd and not be bothered.

"I hate these socials," Hank muttered.

Tracey leaned back against the tree. "You sound just like my grandmother. She'll spend two days putting together a meal for whatever holiday our family is celebrating, and then complain because everyone shows up. But we all know it's just a game with her. She loves having her family around her."

Hank was silent for a moment, then he mumbled, "Yeah, well, havin' my family here is good. They drive me crazy, but life would be damn borin' without them."

"I used to spend a lot of time at Grandma's house after school and during the summer." Tracey smiled at the memories. "She's the best cook in the whole world. Unfortunately, it's not a skill that I inherited or absorbed by association. Even though I watched her cook everything from ten-layer wedding cakes, to pot roast that's so tender it falls off your fork, to a pantry full of fresh peach jam, I can barely boil water."

"Oh, no! Not another woman that can't cook!" Hank exclaimed in mock horror. "What's this world comin' to?"

Tracey laughed, feeling completely comfortable with this old man. And apparently he felt the same because gradually his guard dropped, and he even talked to her about his wife and his wildcatting days back when the rich Texas oil fields were still undisturbed prairies.

Serena returned more than a quarter of an hour later. Without the drinks.

"You can stop by any time and visit me," Hank informed Tracey with a regal air that Tracey suspected was put on for Serena's benefit.

Serena seemed nervous. "Care to join the party, Hank?" She offered her arm.

"Nonsense. I can manage."

Instinctively, Tracey reached for him when he tried to stand. She half expected a refusal, but didn't get one.

"I'll jus' take the arm of this here young thing. You're not attached, are you, honey?"

She smiled. "Only to you, sir."

Hank slapped his leg. "Well, I'll be, a lady with good taste. Glad to have you to brighten things up, young 'un. Yep. Glad, indeed."

A catering company had started serving from long tables covered by white cloths.

"If this is Crystal Creek's idea of a little get-together," Tracey said to Serena, "I can't wait for them to roll out the red carpet for a large party."

"They do things right here at the Double C," Serena agreed.

"Back in the old days, we had real parties here," Hank grumbled. "Ladies would wear dresses and men would wear suit coats and fancy ties."

Serena and Tracey exchanged smiles.

"If it wasn't for that Beverly, we'd never see a dress nowadays."

Tracey glanced around. Sure enough, Beverly was the only one wearing a skirt.

"You girls just live in them trousers."

"They're comfortable," Serena said.

"Yeah, mebbe so, but a man sure don't get to see as much leg as he used to." Wickedness lit his eyes. "Shame. Cryin' shame."

Tracey stayed with Hank through the buffet line, which he insisted he could manage himself. Serena had Cal, and almost everyone else seemed paired up, too.

And there was still no sign of Manny. Tracey and Hank sat at a table for six, and were soon joined by Cal, Serena, Jeff Harris's brother, Scott, and Scott's wife, Valerie. Scott owned the Hole in the Wall Dude Ranch, where the new boot shop was.

As the night wore on, candles were lit, filling the area with a romantic glow. A band began to set up, tuning their instruments to the background of cicadas and crickets.

When the musicians were ready, J. T. McKinney took the microphone. "I hope everyone is having a good time tonight." The guests roared their approval and J.T. continued. "Well, I have one more special treat for y'all tonight. Ms. Jessica Reynolds has agreed to sing for us."

A very attractive woman with flaming red hair billowing around her sequin-covered shoulders stepped onto the small makeshift stage amid thunderous applause. Almost instantly, she launched into a toe-tapping song. Couples moved onto a concrete pad that had been cleared of tables and chairs.

"If you'll excuse us," Cal said, taking Serena by the hand. Scott and Val followed their lead and strolled to the dance floor.

"Help me over to my house, would you, girl?" Hank asked when only the two of them remained at the table. "All this racket's givin' me a headache."

Tracey smiled. Hank and her grandmother would make quite a pair...if they didn't kill each other first.

He leaned on her arm a little more heavily than before as they crossed the lawn and made their way to the porch of a little house not far from the main ranch house.

"I meant what I said." Hank gave Tracey a piercing look. "I won't mind settin' on the porch with you and talkin' some more another day."

"I'd enjoy it, too," Tracey responded. "I'll be sure to come back real soon."

Tracey made her way back to the party, which was still thriving under the sprawling oak trees. Even more couples had crowded into the dancing area, where Jessica was keeping everyone entertained.

"Did he have you for dinner?"

She jumped, then turned around to face the man who'd sauntered through her thoughts all night. Manny.

"Who?" she asked, not really sure what question she was answering.

"Hank," Manny said. "He's notorious for eating mere mortals at every meal. Some say it's his secret to longevity."

Tracey grinned. "Hank's not bad. In fact, he was a real sweetheart."

Manny whistled. "You must have made quite an impression on the old coot."

"I doubt it. I'm not the type who makes an impression."

"Don't underestimate yourself, Tracey. You made quite an impression on me."

He hadn't moved any closer, but the world suddenly seemed to have shrunk. The music receded farther into the background and the moonlight appeared brighter.

"Dance?"

"I'd love to."

They moved toward the dance floor, and Tracey noticed Jessica had segued into a very intimate ballad.

Manny took Tracey into his arms and held her close, but not excessively so. Just close enough so that his sexy scent filled her nostrils and his proprietary touch sent ripples of anticipation skipping along her nerve endings.

"So, did you manage to get all your boxes unpacked this afternoon?" he asked, his breath hot against her ear.

Not exactly the question she'd been expecting...or wanting. "They're multiplying like rabbits, I swear. I open one, and two more take its place. It's odd, because it took me and my parents only two days to pack everything, and it'll take at least two weeks to unpack it."

"Sorry I got hung up at another table for dinner."

"Not to worry. It's not like we had a date or anything."

"Still, I didn't mean to abandon you."

She felt a slow flush begin to work its way up her neck. "I heard you were talking business."

"It got a little more complicated than that. I looked for you to tell you I was disappearing for a few minutes. A very panicky llama tangled with some barbed wire, and I got called out to help."

"A llama and a deer in two days. Quite a weekend."

"At least it's never boring."

"How's Sweetie?"

"She's getting around a little better. I checked on her before I picked you up. In no time, she'll be back out dodging cars."

"That's probably closer to the truth than I want to admit."

"Maybe she learned her lesson." He glanced at the tray of dirty plates that a waiter was carrying away. "I don't suppose there's any food left."

"Enough to feed a small nation."

"Typical McKinney party."

"They do this a lot?"

"At the drop of a hat, if you'll excuse the cliché."

When the song ended, Manny led her from the dance floor and straight to the buffet table. He grabbed a plate, filled it, got Tracey some punch and led her to a secluded table.

"Bubba was telling me it went well in Austin this afternoon," Tracey said as she watched him butter a steaming ear of corn on the cob. "He said he bought that quarter horse."

Manny nodded. "He's proud of Flying Wind."

"So I gathered."

"She's a pretty horse. I'm not sure I would have paid that much for her, but who am I to say? I'm not in the horse business. Probably just as well."

"Was there anything wrong with her?"

"Nothing physical that I could see," Manny said. "But I just have a hunch Bubba's too interested in getting involved in this new business."

"A mistake?"

"Like I said, it's probably a good thing I'm sticking with veterinary medicine. Maybe I don't have the eye for excellent horseflesh."

Tracey sipped the punch, noting that the drink had more than a little bit of a kick. "I'd think your eye would be well trained."

"I'm not that familiar with the racing world, so maybe I'm missing something." Manny pushed aside his plate and sat back, resting his shoulders against the chair. "But I think Bubba could have gotten a better deal, if he'd kept shopping."

"Maybe he was anxious to get started and will be more frugal with other purchases. He sounds like he has it all carefully planned."

"I guess that's all that matters," Manny agreed. "Anyway, he'll probably make a mint and show me."

At a request from J.T., Jessica dedicated "Somewhere other than the Night" to all the young and old lovers in Crystal Creek.

"How 'bout it, Trace? Up for another turn around the dance floor?"

"Are you sure your toes are up to it?" she teased, referring to her last spin around the floor with him.

At least he'd been polite enough not to mention the couple of times she'd tangled with his feet.

"I'll manage, even if I have to hop for a week."

They moved onto the concrete pad, along with nearly thirty other couples. There was little room to actually try out any fancy dance steps, but the crowd forced an intimacy that Tracey found very comfortable.

All too soon, the evening came to an end. The party started to break up, and Tracey and Manny said their good-nights to their hosts. Tyler, J.T.'s oldest son and Cal's brother, strolled over just as Manny and Tracey reached the parking area.

Shaking Manny's hand, Tyler said, "Thanks for helping out earlier. We're much obliged."

"No problem," Manny replied.

Turning to Tracey, Tyler smiled. "I haven't had a chance, but I want to add my welcome to you. Any friend of Serena's has got to be terrific."

Tracey shrugged. "I don't know about the terrific part. But I do think I'm going to feel right at home here."

He stayed for a few more minutes, talking mostly about his venture into wine making and his own special woman, Ruth, before other departing guests forced him to move away.

In the truck as they drove toward town, Manny flicked a glance in Tracey's direction.

"Well, what's your first impression of Crystal Creek and its residents?"

She thought for a moment, searching for the right word to describe the experience. She finally settled on *overwhelming*.

He chuckled. "I know the feeling. That was real similar to my first experience when I moved here a few years ago. Crystal Creek is like one big happy family."

"But I felt like an insider, not an outsider."

"That's because of your connection with the McKinneys. Serena's going to be part of the family before too long."

"How about you?"

"I was needed," Manny said simply. "Good vets are hard to find. I've worked diligently and gone above and beyond. I've proven myself. Around here, what you do counts for almost as much as who you are."

From the way Manny's large, tanned hands tightened on the steering wheel, Tracey could feel that "fitting in" was very important to him.

Back at Señora Sanchez's house, he walked Tracey up the steps that led to the garage apartment, then stopped at the door. She took out her key, half hoping, half fearing he'd kiss her.

He didn't even try.

"Good night, Trace." The tips of his fingers gently feathered her hair back from her face. Then he flicked the blunted end of a fingernail across her lower lip as he repeated the phrase she had heard so often today. "Welcome to Crystal Creek."

He dazzled her with one last, extremely sexy smile, then turned and jogged down the steps. From inside her front room window, Tracey watched as he drove away.

SERENA SNUGGLED into Cal's chest and felt right at home there. He draped an arm around her shoulder as they sat side by side on a swing beneath the Texas sky. The caterers had long since departed, taking with them a truckload of dirty dishes. More than an hour ago, the final guests had made their way to their cars, and most of the McKinney family were already in bed.

"Well?" Serena said. "How do you think Tracey fit in?"

"Wonderfully, as you guessed she would."

"I think she made a great impression, particularly with your great-grandfather. And it takes a minor miracle to accomplish that feat."

"He was taken," Cal granted. "Grandpa Hank must have learned something from his recent scare. Maybe he's getting to be less and less of a curmudgeon."

Simultaneously, they both shook their heads, then laughed.

Night sounds surrounded them as the horses shifted and settled for the night in their corrals and owls called their eerie greetings from their invisible perches in the trees. By the surreal glow of a full moon, the half-melted ice sculpture of a rearing horse took on a ghostly shimmer.

"I introduced Beverly to Tracey. Bev promised to drop by and order some new boots," Serena said.

"Fantastic. She'll be as good a salesman for the La Herencia Boot Stores as I will," Cal declared. "Beverly's endorsement will reap us more profits than a full-page ad in the newspaper."

"My thoughts exactly."

"And it'll cost a hell of a lot less, too."

She felt Cal press a kiss to her forehead. The future looked good for her and Cal and their boot shops. Life didn't get much better. Not by a long shot.

CHAPTER FIVE

MARY GIBSON couldn't sleep. She slipped from the bed, careful not to wake her husband. He'd been out late, negotiating another deal of some sort. She didn't want to let her insomnia disturb his needed rest.

After dressing in the dark, she jotted a note so he wouldn't worry if he woke to find her gone, then drove the deserted roads toward the Longhorn Coffee Shop. As she'd guessed, Nora was already on duty, getting things ready for the rush that would hit before and after church.

"Another cup?" Nora offered, carrying the coffeepot to the table where Mary sat.

"Thanks."

Nora filled Mary's cup, then poured one for herself. After putting the pot back on the burner, she returned to the table.

"Another bad night?" Nora asked sympathetically.

Mary nodded.

"Your hands are trembling," Nora noted.

Mary looked at her hands, verifying what Nora said. As always, Nora's perceptiveness was right on the mark. "I'm worried," she admitted. The words were difficult for Mary to speak. She was generally a loner and her mother had taught her to keep her troubles to herself. But somehow, Nora's sympathetic tone encouraged Mary to open up.

"You've been through some rough times," Mary continued softly. "How did you manage?"

"Friends help. It's nice to know you're not alone. I'm here for you, Mary. I'd like to listen."

"Al's a good man," Mary began, but she noticed a shuttered expression on Nora's face. It wasn't the first time she'd seen negative reactions at the mention of her husband's name. People always seemed to think the worst of Al. She had to admit that sometimes he came on a little strong or acted a bit too coarsely. But it was just his nature. He liked having a good time and playing the big shot. And lately, he had a tendency to jump on any get-rich-quick scheme that ever crossed his mind. After all the years they'd been married, Mary knew Al better than anyone else did, and she understood that his intentions were good . . . it was just that his luck—or his timing—was always bad.

Embarrassed, she glanced around. "We've run into some financial problems." The words nearly stuck in her throat. Here she was, airing her dirty linens in front of the world.

"There's no one here but us," Nora said gently. "And I swear with all my heart that not a word goes beyond this table."

Mary took a long drink from her coffee, feeling it warm the numbness inside.

"In this day and age, it's rare to find someone who hasn't experienced some financial troubles. Particularly in your and Bubba's line of work. It's nothing to be ashamed of."

"Well, Al is bound and determined to see us through this...."

"But?" Nora prompted.

"But he's speculating with money we can't afford to lose."

Nora nodded.

"Neither of us knows anything about the horse racing business. And it's an expensive gamble." Mary felt as though a huge weight had been lifted from her shoulders. To actually give voice to her concerns made them seem less burdensome.

"Are you getting any professional input?"

"He's being smart about it," Mary admitted. "He had a meeting with a potential partner in Austin last night. The man runs several of his own horses, evidently with success."

Mary became lost in her own thoughts for a minute or two, as she considered the pile of bills on the kitchen table and the rapidly dwindling bank balance. She didn't understand horse racing, but she couldn't see how it could possibly pay off quickly enough to save their ranch.

"Things have a way of working out," Nora said. "I'm not saying you shouldn't be concerned at all, but together you might be all right. Talk to Bubba, tell him how you feel."

Mary's mouth dropped. "I couldn't let him know I don't trust him!"

Nora's neatly penciled eyebrows lifted.

"He's a good provider," Mary assured Nora, defending the silent accusation. "I can't turn on him now."

"That's not turning on him, honey," Nora said, reaching over and patting Mary's hand. "Maybe you can actually help him. It's amazing what a little teamwork can accomplish."

Mary smiled. "Maybe you're right," she agreed.

While Nora left to take care of another early-rising couple, Mary finished her coffee. Perhaps things weren't as bad as she'd thought. After all, she'd known for years that Allan Gibson was a good man at heart.

BUBBA KNEW the instant his wife left the bed.

He'd lain awake with his eyes closed until he heard the front door shut behind her.

After her car started and the engine faded into the early-dawn air, Bubba climbed from beneath the sheet and adjusted the waistband of his pajamas. He figured Mary hadn't gone far. He knew her well enough to be confident of that.

Sure enough, a note lay on the dresser. He picked up the paper, reflecting that the script was every bit as feminine as Mary herself. He read it, and experienced a moment of panic that she was heading for the Longhorn Coffee Shop. After all, he'd had breakfast there yesterday with Billy Jo. Yesterday and a whole lot of other days, too.

For a minute, he considered jumping in his pickup and following Mary to the Longhorn, but dismissed the idea. She trusted him. It was her greatest asset and her greatest fault. But her trust could prove his greatest ally. Even if Nora told all, Mary wouldn't believe a word of it. And if she did, well, she'd be hurt, but she'd forgive him. Her daddy had had a wandering eye, too. That hadn't stopped her parents from having a long, relatively happy marriage.

In his heart, it was important to him to be a good husband. Mary deserved it. He'd struggled to suppress his roving eye, and had even turned to J.T. for advice. But nothing helped. The harder Bubba tried to stay away from the ladies, the more the compulsion to seek them out grew. He was addicted. He wasn't proud of it, but there it was.

Yet, in almost every other way, he was a good husband. Except that their finances had gone to hell in a bad way in the past few months. Bubba looked out the back window in the direction of the barn where Flying Wind had spent the night. He couldn't help but feel a sense of trepidation mixed with anticipation that things would work out. They simply *had* to. Mary didn't have a clue just how bad "bad" was. Bubba aimed to keep it that way.

His gaze was still riveted on the barn. Flying Wind was their ticket to financial security. And that, Bubba Gibson *would* provide. No matter the cost.

Bubba shivered, though there was no chill in the air. Nope. No cost was too high to save his ranch.

"GETTING SETTLED is taking forever," Tracey commented, as she glanced toward several boxes that hadn't yet been touched. And she'd spent all Sunday and this morning unpacking.

"It's already beginning to look more like home," Serena said.

"If I ever find a hammer and nails, it'll look even better. So far, only the necessities have been uncovered. I just didn't realize I had so many things I can't live without.''

They shared a laugh.

"But I have to admit to loving the place,'' Tracey continued. "It has a lot of character. The sloped ceilings are great.''

"I was hoping you'd like it.''

"Are you kidding? You couldn't have chosen a better place for me,'' she told her friend. "And Señora Sanchez is a wonderful landlady.''

Tracey followed Serena back into the living room. Tracey hadn't slept much the night before, despite being exhausted from the weekend. She'd given up trying, sometime after dawn, and climbed out of bed. After a shower and half a pot of coffee, she hadn't felt any better.

Though she'd never admit it to Serena, Tracey knew Manny was partly responsible for her sleeplessness. His scent, his touch, their dance, had brought old feelings back to life, feelings she'd thought were long dead.

Tracey had searched him out at church yesterday morning, before realizing that his heritage made it unlikely he attended a Southern Baptist service. Strangely, though, she'd missed him.

"Earth calling.''

Tracey dragged her thoughts back to the conversation with Serena.

"Are you sure you don't need another day before you report to work? I can cover today if you need the afternoon off. You look exhausted."

"I missed two days last week while I packed and loaded the trailer. I'm definitely ready to get back to my *real* job."

"You're so dedicated," Serena teased.

"Well, there won't be any business left if we don't get busy."

Serena and Tracey walked down the stairs to Serena's car.

Serena had promised to give Tracey a ride the first day, so she could acquaint her with the layout of the town. Besides, Tracey's car wasn't ready yet at the garage.

On the way down one of the main streets, she couldn't help but notice Manny's official office...and the fact that his pickup truck was parked outside. Unbidden, thoughts of their time together returned.

"Trace?"

"Sorry," she said, feeling a little guilty for not paying attention. "What did you say?"

"You really are distracted today. Are you sure you're okay?"

"Just fine." She held up a hand in mock surrender. "Promise."

Only a few minutes later, they arrived at the Hole in the Wall. After passing several guest cabins, a huge barn, a pool and some tennis courts, they stopped in front of a building that looked like the main street of an Old West town. Several businesses were housed behind the aged wood storefronts. Nestled between a beauty shop and a general store was the La Herencia Boot Store. A large picture window was painted with boots in various sizes, shapes and colors, and the business hours were prominently displayed on the door.

"Here's your set of keys," Serena said. "Go ahead and try them. We didn't check them after the locksmith cut them last week."

Excitement surged through Tracey. The key turned and a brass cowbell jumped and clanged when she opened the front door. Pausing just inside, she looked around. This was what she loved best.

The familiar scent of tooled leather filled her nose as she sucked in a deep, eager breath. The boutique was larger than she'd pictured when discussing plans with Cal and Serena. It dwarfed their other location in Wolverton. The selection of handmade boots that lined the walls was incredible, beyond Tracey and Serena's wildest dreams in their less-than-auspicious beginnings.

"I have great hopes for this store," Serena said. "Something to do with Cal being a local celebrity, I guess. With you here now, it's going to go like gangbusters," she continued. "Managing's not my strong point. And I'd like to spend some time developing a few new ideas I have."

For the next hour, they went over the books, projections for the next year's growth, inventory statistics and ideas for new merchandising strategies. Serena outlined the status of all the special orders and the more interesting quirks of some of their customers, and showed Tracey where the order sheets and other files were kept.

The business was, indeed, bigger and better than Tracey had imagined, but she welcomed the challenge, and knew she could handle it. After all, she and Serena had survived the lean years before Cal McKinney had become a part of their picture.

"Well," said Serena finally, "what do you think?"

Tracey looked around. Then she smiled. "I think this is what I was born for."

She and Serena exchanged swift looks. "Me, too," her partner confessed.

After saying goodbye and promising to return later in the day, Serena headed for the door. Once there, she paused, hand curved around the brass knob. "Well, Ms. Cotter, it looks as though we've finally arrived."

Tracey couldn't have agreed more.

AT WHAT WAS SUPPOSED to be closing time, Tracey blew a puff of air upward, trying to cool herself off. It had been a long first day on the job. There was a lot of work to be done here.

She thrived on the challenge, but her back didn't. It ached from all the bending and stretching she'd had to do to arrange the stock and deal with a large delivery of supplies.

"I like what you've done with the displays," Serena said, joining Tracey near the front counter. "It has a lot more visual appeal than what I put together. My eye's not nearly as good as yours."

"I'm glad you approve. I've had two orders for those turquoise-colored boots just today."

"Those?" Serena asked, pointing.

"Yep."

"I didn't sell a single pair of them. I was going to recommend you discontinue them."

"It's all in the merchandising," Tracey said.

"Or the management."

"Must be the management," Tracey agreed.

"Or the merchandising."

They both laughed.

"You've certainly got the talent—no doubt about it."

"None of my talents would matter diddly without your designs."

"This mutual admiration society stuff is great!"

Tracey slipped into the back and grabbed a diet soda for each of them from the small refrigerator. Then she dropped onto the bench seat, padded for customer comfort.

"Did the rest of the day go as well?" Serena inquired.

Tracey inclined her head to one side. "Better than that, actually. I think the orders will show business was up today."

Serena stood behind the counter and popped the lid on her drink. "I think moving you here was a great idea."

"Now if we can work out the problems in the other stores..." Tracey said. She took a long drink from the can to relieve her parched throat. She'd worked all the way through lunch, and hadn't taken a break until the last customer left just before Serena arrived.

"If we don't find someone good for the Wolverton store, I'm afraid it'll go out of business. But we can't afford to just have you baby-sit it. This one demands more of our attention."

"I agree. But I'd hate to see it die for lack of good management."

"Ideas?"

"Maybe bring one of the assistants here from Wolverton, let her work here with me, then transfer her back in a managerial position."

"Might work," Serena said. "I'll run it by Cal."

Hearing a knock on the door, Tracey glanced up. All she could see beneath the Closed sign was a pair of Texas-mud brown boots and denim-encased legs. "No rest for the wicked. Silly me, I was actually hoping to make it home sometime tonight."

"I'll grab it. Hate to turn away potential business."

"Me, too," Tracey agreed.

"Go ahead and finish with the books."

"It's a deal." Tracey disappeared into the back room as the brass cowbell jumped musically.

A few seconds later, she heard Serena behind her. "What's up?" she asked her tall, thin friend.

"The customer out front refuses to deal with anyone but you."

"Me? Why me? I've only been here a day."

"Don't know," Serena replied. "Where are you with the day's records?"

"I balanced, first try, thankfully."

"I'm green with envy. Accounting drives me crazy."

Tracey put the print-out on the shelf and pointed to a stack of checks and cash.

"I've started the deposit slip."

"Great. Go ahead, I'll finish."

Tracey traded places with her partner, then walked back out to the showroom. "Manny!"

The grin he gave her with was enough to make her insides take a dive. "Seems I ruined my boots Friday night. Got any suggestions?"

"Several, actually."

"Great." His eyes flashed as he pretended to misinterpret her comment.

Tracey felt her cheeks color hotly as all sorts of thoughts tumbled through her mind. She gave him a wry reprimanding look and began listing ways to restore his boots, all of which he discounted. "Are you being intentionally difficult?"

"No." That grin again. "Yeah, maybe."

His smile was contagious.

"Did I hear you've got a difficult customer on your hands, partner?" Serena asked, joining them.

" 'Fraid so."

"Do you suppose he couldn't read the Closed sign?"

"I think he ignored it on purpose." Tracey looked up at Manny, but her teasing turned to something quite different . . . and dangerous, as she saw the raw sexuality burning in his eyes.

"Maybe he doesn't realize I've got a date with one Cal McKinney that I don't want to miss," Serena continued, pretending to be unaware of the silent exchange between her two friends.

"Don't let me keep you," Manny said.

"But I need to take Tracey home." Serena glanced at her watch. "Don't worry. I'm not late. Yet."

"Go on ahead. I'll take Trace home when we're finished."

"Oh!" Serena looked from one to the other, then slid Tracey a sly wink. Her friend was actually matchmaking, Tracey realized with a start. Serena had said nothing earlier about a date with Cal. In fact, she and Tracey were supposed to get together tonight for a long-overdue girls' night.

"In that case, I'll be on my way. Good night."

" 'Night," Tracey said.

"She's transparent," Manny commented when the door jangled behind Serena.

"That obvious, huh?"

"Yep."

"And you weren't?" she teased.

"All right, maybe we're both guilty as charged. Can't blame a guy, though, when he spent half of Sunday morning in Mass praying for deliverance from obsessive thoughts."

His words startled her.

"Then spent the rest of the day making up reasons to see you again," he went on as he took a step closer. "Boots seemed like a natural excuse."

"You could have just asked." He was so close she could smell his musky after-shave and feel the heat of his body.

"Would you have agreed?"

"Yes," she breathed.

"In that case, after selling me a pair of boots, how about having dinner with me?" He reached up and, with the tip of his finger, followed the curve of her hair where she had tucked it behind her ear. His touch lingered on her neck for a moment, and his grin softened as his gaze fell to her lips.

"I'd love to."

Tracey was beginning to think she'd do anything to be rewarded with that grin...and that touch...and that mouth....

"AL, THERE'S SOMETHING I want to discuss with you."

Bubba wadded his napkin and tossed it on his thoroughly cleaned plate, in preparation for rising from the table.

"Please don't get up and leave just yet," Mary said softly. "We truly do need to talk."

Bubba paused in the middle of sliding his chair back. He looked at her and frowned. She had an unreadable expression on her face. Uncomfortably, he remembered she'd seen Nora at the Longhorn that morning.

"I went out for a little while this morning and had the opportunity to do some thinking."

She took a sip of her iced tea and Bubba felt a knot in his throat. He loosened his string tie. If Nora had been putting notions in his Mary's head...

"I know we've been experiencing some financial strain lately... now, Al, don't be denying it."

She patted his hand in that maternal way that drove him crazy. "It's not that bad, sugar," he said placatingly, hoping she couldn't see through the easy denial. Actually, in all their years of marriage, he infrequently lied. And when he did, the sin was generally one of omission. "We might be going through a rough spell, but it'll pass."

"But there's no reason you should have to deal with it all by yourself, Al. Marriage is a partnership. I can't let you carry the load all by yourself. It wouldn't be right. It wouldn't be right at all."

"Sugar, my job is to take care of you and I intend to do just that."

"I've been thinking...."

He couldn't take the suspense. "Yes?"

"Maybe I should get a job."

Bubba's chair toppled over backward as he lurched to his feet. "You've been thinking what!" he demanded. Bubba didn't care that his voice thundered across all eight thousand acres of the

Flying Horse. Nor did he care if any of the few remaining ranch hands overheard him. "Listen to me, Mary Gibson. We haven't been married for thirty-some years for you to talk about going and getting a job! I won't hear of it, do you understand me?"

"Al, please settle down. There's no sense getting your spurs in a spin."

He felt the blood pound at his temples. He hadn't been this angry in more years than he cared to remember. And never had his anger been directed toward his soft-spoken, kindhearted wife. Until now.

"Your blood pressure must be going through the ceiling. Now take it easy, Al."

She hadn't so much as raised her eyes to meet his gaze. Her voice stayed steady, even though his temper was soaring.

"Sit down, Al. Let's discuss this like adults."

"I'm not discussing anything that involves your name and a job in the same sentence. Things are not that bad, and I swear to you I won't let them get that bad. No wife of mine is ever going to have to work outside this ranch. I'm the man of this household...."

"But any help I provide will get us back on our feet that much faster."

"That is not the point," he said, pointing an index finger at her.

"I'm sure Nora could use some extra help at the Longhorn. In fact, I spoke with her just this morning about maybe..."

"Waitressing! Hell no, Mary. Don't you even go thinking 'bout something like that. Hell no."

"Don't curse under my roof, Allan Gibson. I won't stand for it. Besides, there's nothing wrong with waitressing. It's an honest profession."

He leaned forward, fingers gripped tightly around the table's edge, more convinced than ever that he'd sell his soul to provide for Mary. "I said no, Mary, and I meant it. Do I make myself clear?"

He noticed a sheen of tears in her eyes, but he refused to be dissuaded. He'd rather sell the ranch than sell his wife. And in his mind having her work was tantamount to selling her.

"You make yourself clear, Allan."

She met his gaze solidly, so solidly it nearly unnerved him.

"I was just trying to help," she added.

"Don't," he said. "This is my worry, Mary, not yours. And you have my word I won't let you down."

With that, he grabbed his hat, shoved it on his head and slammed out the back door.

CHAPTER SIX

SILENTLY, Manny walked up behind Tracey, placing his hands on her shoulders. "Sorry," he said when she jumped. "Didn't mean to startle you."

She turned in his arms. Her lips had parted in surprise, and he caught a peek of her tongue. He fought to suppress a groan. A gorgeous woman was in his arms, her shoulders invitingly curved in his hands.

"I was just reading these clippings about you." She turned back to the wall. She and Manny were waiting to be seated in the dining room of the dude ranch.

Manny realized he'd been absently moving his fingers over her shoulders. Self-consciously, he stopped.

"Having all these newspaper articles on the wall is a wonderful idea," she said.

"Valerie Harris dreamed it up. All of the pictures and stories are about folks in town."

"Including you."

"Really?" he asked. "I've never taken the time to read them all." He looked over her shoulder, recognizing the article that had appeared when he bought the veterinary practice from ol' Doc Harding a little more than two years ago.

"It says you graduated from A&M with honors."

"So did a lot of people."

She turned again. This time her action brought their bodies together as the tips of her breasts brushed against his chest. His own body reacted immediately to the unintentional stimulus. As he looked down into her wide, intelligent eyes, he wondered how had he ever thought, even for a moment on a dark night, that she was a boy?

Flustered, he took a quick step backward. He was coming to value Tracey's friendship very much. The last thing he wanted to do was to run her off with unwelcome sexual overtures.

"Don't underestimate yourself, Manny. You're obviously very good at your work."

"I try hard, Tracey. Being a veterinarian is the only thing I ever wanted to do."

"Besides playing football."

"Oh, man, I'd forgotten that was mentioned."

Tracey laughed.

"I had a little talent for playing ball, and I used it to accomplish my goal."

"A little talent? This article says you played in two Cotton Bowls and scored the winning touchdown in one of them."

"Any more of my secrets laid bare to the paying public?" He noticed a dimple in her chin that added to her unique beauty, and discovered he was having a hell of a time concentrating on the conversation. What he really wanted was to taste her lips and see if they could possibly be as delicious as they looked.

"Just the name of every cheerleader you ever dated," she teased.

"Nah," he said lightly. "The article wasn't nearly long enough."

"Hernandez! Party of two."

Manny raised a finger, signaling the hostess. She nodded. "Right this way, sir."

He automatically placed his fingers lightly in the small of Tracey's back. He'd done the same thing on dozens of dates, but hadn't realized how proprietary the gesture was.

He held her chair, scooted it in, then took his seat across from her. A candle flickered on the table in an amber-colored glass sconce, providing the ambience he wanted.

The waitress took their orders, then returned a few minutes later with wine.

"This is lovely." Tracey leaned back in her seat. "I don't think there's a muscle in my entire body that doesn't ache after the move and the huge shipment of supplies that arrived this afternoon."

"Sounds like you really needed this break."

"I should be home, putting things away, but I'd much rather be here." *With you,* she added silently. "How's Sweetie doing?"

"She seemed a little more content last night. At least she didn't try to dash past me when I opened the stall door. I think she's decided to enjoy the attention while it lasts."

"Smart lady."

He watched, interested, as Tracey took a sip from the crystal goblet. Her small fingers curved around the stem and the sudden thought of what it would feel like to have her hand curled around him raced through his mind. Manny took a long drink from the water glass, glad when several pieces of ice slipped into his mouth. *Cool down, fella,* he reprimanded himself. *This one's different.*

Time passed too quickly, and the main course dishes were cleared away. The waitress brought the dessert tray, and Manny noticed Tracey eye a slice of cheesecake covered with a quarter inch of bittersweet chocolate.

"It looks sinful," she said. "I really shouldn't have it, though. It'll take at least an hour to exercise all those calories off my hips."

"You've worked hard today. All weekend, as a matter of fact. You deserve to indulge."

The candle lit her eyes with a sparkle of gold. And maybe a hint of mischief. "How about sharing a piece of the cheesecake with me?"

"Share it?"

"Come on, Manny, live a little."

"You talked me into it."

A few minutes later, the plate was placed between them with only a single fork. By the time Manny realized it, the waitress had vanished to parts unknown.

"You first," she offered.

"It's your dessert."

Obviously, she needed no further urging. "Chocolate is my downfall." Tracey sank the fork's prongs into the cheesecake. "Okay, so I'll admit it, I can resist anything but temptation." She closed her mouth around the bite.

She made a slight noise, suspiciously like a moan, as if thoroughly enjoying the experience. He'd heard the same sound before. In bed. But not from her... something he was growing to regret more every minute.

"Decadent." She sighed.

"I'll say." Since when had dessert become such a turn on? he wondered.

She offered him the fork. "You've got to try it, Manny."

He did. The fork was still warm from her mouth and a trace of chocolate had clung to the prongs. He barely noticed the sweet richness of the dessert as he took a bite. He had to get out of here. Soon. Before he pulled her into his arms and licked the chocolate flavor off her lips.

Yet he hesitated taking her back to his house as he would have any number of other dates. He didn't know her that well, but he recognized one thing for sure: Tracey Cotter wasn't the kind of woman for a casual fling.

And if he'd had any doubts about that, Cal and Serena had laid them to eternal rest on their unexpected visit yesterday. They'd made it clear that if his intentions toward Tracey weren't honorable, he'd be dealing with her protectors.

"Up for a little dancing?"

"Sounds fun. If I don't fall asleep on you first."

"I'll take my chances."

He took her to Zack's, with its loud band, mile-long hardwood bar, and high-energy atmosphere. Despite the owner's troubles, the bar was still going strong. It was the safest place he could think of, considering they'd be surrounded by people all evening. Maybe, just maybe, the crowd and the noise would keep him from doing or saying something he might regret later.

FOR THE FIRST TIME in his life, Bubba Gibson felt sick about something he was going to do. He had qualms about tonight, more qualms than he'd thought he would have. More than he should have had.

Resolutely, though, he pushed the queasiness away. A man had to do what a man had to do to provide for his family. Ever since his argument with Mary a little more than a week ago, he'd felt a pressing need to resolve the mess their finances were in—before the bank did something more drastic than send notices.

Last night he'd returned home to Mary, after finding no solace with Billy Jo, and made love to his wife with a tenderness he hadn't felt in years.

Her offer to help had humbled him in some ways. In others, it made him feel less of a man. And he couldn't tolerate that. Since then, though, she'd looked at him confidently, trusting that he'd honor his word and solve their financial crisis. Bubba Gibson wouldn't fail her or the Flying Horse.

Nervously, he kept glancing toward the barn door. It was locked. There was no way anyone could get in. Yet that didn't stop paranoia from nipping at him. "Damn it all to hell, are you sure this will work?"

"Guaranteed," the other man said.

The damned llama made so many noises and skittered around so much, Bubba was convinced someone would hear the racket and come to see what was going on. Especially before they were finished.

"Goddamn it, man, hurry up," Bubba whispered fiercely.

"Patience, Mr. Gibson. Patience. We have a small margin for error. Nevertheless, we don't want anything to go wrong."

"Damn straight."

While the man continued to work, Bubba felt sick. He knew he should call it off, but he was already in too deep. And Mary's face, when she'd offered to work as a waitress, kept haunting him. He'd do it for Mary. For himself. So their future would be secure. And for no other reason.

Before another thirty seconds passed, the llama lay dead.

Maybe, just maybe, Bubba realized, his conscience might not agree with the logical thoughts in his mind. Then he ran to a bucket and vomited.

"DEAD?" MANNY REPEATED the word as he struggled through hundreds of layers of sleep. "Who died?"

"Manny, damn you, wake up!"

He forced open one eye. No matter how long he spent on twenty-four-hour call, he never got accustomed to the phone calls. "I'm awake," he lied. Squinting, he tried to read the digital dial on the clock. Five forty-five. He had to get up soon anyway.

"Manny, it's Bubba."

"Yeah, Bubba?"

"My ranch hand, Luke Harte, just came to the main house and woke me and Mary up. One of my llamas is dead."

"How? When?"

"That's the damnedest thing, there doesn't seem to be any reason why she died. I think maybe you should take a look."

As Bubba spoke, Manny came wide awake. An animal was dead. "All right," he said, jumping out of bed and reaching for the jeans he'd worn the night before. "Hang tight, Bubba. I'll be there in ten minutes."

Not more than three minutes later, Manny was speeding along the nearly deserted roads toward the kind of scene he most detested in his practice.

"IT WAS a record-setting week for customer traffic!" Serena exclaimed Friday evening toward quitting time. "Congratulations, partner. I knew you could do it!"

"Record-setting, really?" Tracey asked. "I knew it had been good, but I didn't have a clue it was that good. In fact, there were two people waiting this morning when I got here. I've been thinking we might want to consider lengthening the store hours."

Tracey was elated, but exhausted. Since eight o'clock, business hadn't let up. She hadn't been able to eat her peanut butter sandwich, and her apple lay on a table in the back room, with only three or four bites missing. She wanted nothing more than to go home, take a hot bath and curl up in front of the television. But there were still a couple of hours' work ahead of her.

"Fine. But we need to talk about the Wolverton store. The problem I mentioned there just seems to be getting worse. I think we're going to take your suggestion and transfer one of the women here to work with you for a while. The current manager just doesn't have an ounce of your flair. In the hour I was there this afternoon, I had three customer complaints. And complaints are the death of a business like ours."

Tracey nodded.

"I'm going to spend some more time there this week, hopefully get things back on track while you train the Wolverton woman. If it doesn't work out, I'll probably have to fire the manager."

"I know how you hate to do that."

"Owning a chain of stores all over the state, being the biggest name in the industry was all I dreamed about for years. I just never stopped to consider all the problems we'd encounter along the way."

"Do you want me to head back there?" Tracey wasn't exactly sure why, but the idea didn't appeal to her at all. In the short time she'd been in Crystal Creek, she'd grown to love it.

"Heavens, no. You've got a great thing going here. I'd hate to see two stores slide."

"If I can do anything, just let me know."

"Just keep up the good work here."

"Actually, there's something I've been meaning to run by you and Cal."

"Sure."

"I know I haven't been here very long, but I've already got a feel for the clientele and what they're looking for."

"You've got a new idea?"

Tracey saw the excitement that lit her partner's eyes. Serena loved the creative opportunities of a new project.

"I'd like to see us expand what we offer at this store."

"What do you have in mind?"

"Bridles, for one."

"Bridles? That's a great idea."

"I was thinking we could do a custom line for the Hole in the Wall's stables. Scott stopped by earlier this week and we did a little brainstorming. We could tool his new logo into the leather."

"That'd take a lot of work," Serena said, skepticism obviously warring with the creative challenge.

"But it would be worth it. Scott said he's willing to commission the first set, and who knows, it might spawn a whole new business."

"I like it," Serena decided. "Do you have something specific in mind?"

"As a matter of fact, I do." Tracey reached under the counter and grabbed her sketch pad. "They're not much, just a rough idea."

"Tracey, these are excellent," Serena said a few minutes later. "I didn't know you had such talent in the art department."

"They're not very good," Tracey protested. "Certainly nothing like what you produce."

"Don't sell yourself short. We could go into production soon with these."

"You really think so?"

"Absolutely. Let me run them by Cal when he gets here—"

"While you're at it, you might want to take a look at the next few pages, also."

Serena did, and let out a long whistle. "When you talk about branching out, you really mean it."

"Too much?"

"No way. This is exactly what I've been looking for." Serena studied the drawings. "Holsters, huh?"

"There's a design on the next page that may work perfectly for undercover cops or detectives— you know, whoever needs to wear a gun under a jacket."

For the next few minutes, they bounced ideas off each other. Serena was obviously thrilled to have her passion stirred. And Tracey was relieved. As a minor partner, she couldn't override Serena's decisions, so it was really gratifying when Serena showed the same kind of enthusiasm for a project that Tracey did.

"Well, Trace, I'd say you hit on a gold mine."

Tracey smiled. "So you'll get to work on the ideas soon?"

"Tonight, okay?"

They shook hands, as they had so many times in the past.

"Look, there was another reason I stopped by today." Serena glanced out the window. "And since Cal should be here soon, I'd like to talk to you privately."

"Sure," Tracey said. They went into the back room. "Sounds serious."

"Not serious, really. Just something I want you to be aware of."

Tracey picked up her apple, then tossed it into the garbage pail. She pushed her hair back from her face, then dragged her fingers through the ends at her nape. For once, she was really grateful for short hair. Even in Texas, autumn wasn't supposed to be so hot. "Well?" she prompted.

It wasn't like Serena to hem and haw. She usually came out and said what she wanted, bluntly, whether it offended people or not.

"All right." Serena sat on a chair, long legs crossed at the knees. "I want to talk to you about Manny."

"Manny?"

"He's a real nice guy. . . ."

"Why am I dreading the million-dollar 'but'?"

"Well, to put it mildly, he's gained quite a reputation with the ladies."

Tracey laughed. "So you've said before."

"I just don't want to see you get hurt. I know what that idiot James did to you."

Tracey winced. If she never heard that name again, it would be a day too soon. "Serena, I appreciate your concern, but there's nothing to worry about. Really. Manny's been nothing but a perfect gentleman with me."

"But how do you feel about him?"

"I don't think it's possible to say how I feel about him. We've gone out a couple of times, but that's all there is to it. Honest. We haven't so much as kissed."

"He *is* being a gentleman," Serena said. "Don't get me wrong, Trace. I'm not warning you to stay away from Manny. He's a great person. Even though he's lived here only a couple of years, he's well liked and respected."

Tracey smiled. "You're talking out of both sides of your mouth. On one hand, you warn me not to get too close, then you provide a detailed synopsis of all his good qualities."

"I know." Serena sighed. "I want to see you happy. But safe."

"I appreciate your concern. I felt protective over you when you met Cal."

Serena stood and brushed imaginary wrinkles from her pressed denim jeans when the tinkle of the cowbell attached to the front door informed them that either Cal had arrived, or they had yet another customer.

It was both. Cal walked in with Beverly beside him.

"Hi, Cal...Beverly," Tracey said, emerging from the back room.

Beverly smiled. "I've been meaning to get by here sooner, but Jeff and Hank's new business is keeping me so busy."

"Hi, hon," Serena said. "Just wait until you see the new ideas Tracey has come up with."

"Impressive?"

"Extremely."

"Good."

"I was wondering if you were serious about custom-designing a pair of boots for me," Beverly said, addressing both Tracey and Serena.

"Absolutely," Tracey said. "That's what makes us different from everyone else. We can do any design."

Beverly smiled secretively. "How about oil wells?"

"Oil wells?" Cal asked.

Beverly nodded. "With oil gushing out the top."

"Hank was telling me all about the oil well at the party the other night," Tracey commented. "He said no one but Jeff had believed him...."

"All right, all right," Cal said, holding up his arms as if in surrender. "We've admitted it. We were wrong."

"Your loss," Beverly stated, though her wink left no doubt she was teasing.

"Remember the rest of us now that you're rich and famous, cuz," Cal said.

"I've been rich and famous my entire life."

"Infamous," Cal corrected with a grin.

"And I haven't forgotten you yet."

The interchange amused Tracey, but she was quick to get down to business.

"Have you ever bought boots from us before?" she asked, starting to fill out a custom-order sheet.

"No."

"Okay, we'll need to have last models made of your feet and we'll keep them on record."

"Oh, they're not for me," Beverly said. "They're a surprise for Jeff."

"That's a lovely idea," Tracey said.

"His birthday's in three weeks. Is that a problem?"

"Not for family," Serena said.

"Great. I brought along an old pair of boots. Can we use them?"

"That'll work." Serena nodded. "Are they in the car?"

"In the trunk. Cal wouldn't let me put them in the back where I was going to." She wrinkled her nose.

"And when you get a whiff of them, you won't blame me," Cal said.

Within the next few minutes, the store was getting crowded again, despite the fact that the closing hour had come and gone. Val and Scott stopped by, and everyone greeted one another warmly.

"We saw your car, Cal, and thought we'd drop in and see how everything's going. Business living up to your expectations?" Scott looked at Tracey for the answer.

"Better than that," Tracey said.

"That's great. Say, Tracey, have you had an opportunity to discuss that idea for those custom bridles with Serena?"

"She has," Serena said. "And it's a great idea. I'll get busy on providing a sample, based on Tracey's designs."

"Bridles?" Cal said.

"You're going to love it, honey," Serena assured him.

"I could use a new bridle for Dandi," Beverly supplied.

"There you go," Tracey said to her partners, "built-in buyers, before the product even hits the shelves."

"Everything should be this easy," Serena said. "Mind if I take your sketch pad home so I can get to work right away?"

"You've got your work cut out for you this weekend," Tracey said. "Let me know if you need any help."

"Scott, you got any plans?" Cal asked with an exaggerated pout. "Seems I'm alone this weekend."

"All my horses are getting checkups this weekend. Manny's going to stop by and start on them within the next hour."

At the mention of Manny's name, Tracey's pulse gave an inadvertent leap. But she sternly told herself to get a grip. Manny wasn't even her usual type. Certainly he wasn't a thing like the minister's son, Bryce... or James.

"You know how long that can take," Scott continued. "We could still be at it Monday morning. If I finish before then, I have football tickets for Sunday afternoon."

"Sorry," Valerie said to her husband, "but you're stuck taking me. I wouldn't miss that game for anything. Besides, I want to collect your fifty dollars on the spot."

"No chance. You'd better bring your purse, honey, because I intend to clean you out."

"Poor, lonesome Cal," Beverly said unsympathetically to her cousin. "Looks like you're out of luck."

"You don't understand. If I don't find somewhere to disappear to, Serena will put me to work."

They all laughed, and Tracey experienced a pang of being an outsider, even though everyone attempted to make her feel welcome.

When she thought the store already bulged at the seams, another car pulled up. At this rate, Tracey figured she'd be home in time for breakfast.

"Well, I'll be. It's Tyler and Ruth," Cal said unnecessarily. "Maybe they want bridles, too," he suggested teasingly to Serena.

Tyler and Ruth walked in together, both smiling as if sharing a secret.

"Hi, all," Tyler said, his arm casually draped around Ruth's shoulders. She looked at him adoringly.

Must be the water, Tracey told herself. There was no other possible explanation for all the love she saw around her.

"Where the hell have you been?" Cal asked. "I haven't seen you in a few days."

"We just got back from seeing Daddy and Cynthia at the Double C. Daddy said I could find you here."

"Is there something going on I should be aware of?"

Again, Ruth and Tyler exchanged a conspiratorial glance. The silence in the shop became palpable.

"You want to tell, them darlin'?" Tyler asked.

"Tell us what?" Cal demanded.

"Or shall I?" Ty taunted, drawing out the suspense. He'd always enjoyed teasing his younger siblings.

"Tell us what?" Cal demanded again.

"We were staying at Ruth's place in California."

"And?" Cal prompted, when Tyler trailed off. He looked back and forth between the two, as if ready to shake their secret out of them.

"We eloped."

No one said a word. Everyone just stared at the obviously ecstatic couple.

"Meet Mrs. Tyler McKinney," Tyler said proudly, raising his bride's hand to his lips.

After the stunned silence, a cacophony of sound erupted. Ruth and Tyler accepted everyone's sincere best wishes and congratulations. There was a lot of back slapping for Tyler and warm hugs for Ruth.

A few minutes later things finally settled down enough for Beverly to demand explanations.

"I finally convinced her to have me," Tyler said. "Man oh man, did it take a lot of work."

"Stop," Ruth said. "It was just a matter of convincing you of the errors of your ways."

"Errors? Of my ways?"

"So why the hell did you elope?" Cal demanded, interrupting what appeared to be a private discussion. "Kids elope, not grown adults."

"These ones did," Ty boasted.

"That's not the way things are done around here, brother. You, more than anyone else, know that. And should respect that. Everyone wants to share in the festivities."

"We didn't want to lay this responsibility on J.T.," Ruth said.

"He's feeling a lot better," Cal said. "You know he enjoyed the shindig last week. Said it breathed new life into the place."

"Planning a wedding's a lot different than a shindig," Ruth said firmly. "We thought the excitement might have been too much for him. And, Cynthia doesn't need half of Crystal Creek traipsing through her house now that she's in the family way. Maybe we were feeling a little over-protective of them both."

"The real truth is, we didn't want to wait another minute," Tyler said. He kissed Ruth on the forehead. "I couldn't risk her changing her mind on me."

"You need a reception now," Scott said, apparently thinking along the same lines as Cal.

"Right," Cal said.

"If you don't want to use the Double C, I'll be happy to host it here at Hole in the Wall. We've got the facilities."

Tyler shook his head. "We really appreciate the generosity, Scott. But I'm afraid we've already made plans."

"Plans?" Cal asked.

"We're going on a honeymoon."

"We'll have the reception after you get back," Val supplied.

"We'll be gone quite a while," Ruth said. "Since it's not the kind of trip we plan on taking real often."

"Just where are you going?" Beverly asked.

"France."

"France?" everyone seemed to echo.

"For how long?" Cal asked.

"You're full of more questions than Dad and Cynthia," Tyler said good-naturedly. "Even old Grandpa Hank wasn't as obnoxious as you. We're planning to combine business with pleasure, checking out the competition, so to speak, of the French vineyards."

"We're leaving in the morning," Ruth supplied. "And we won't be back until late next month."

"In that case, I think we should at least have a drink and toast your happiness in the lounge," Scott said.

Ruth and Tyler looked at each other.

"Oh, come on," Serena said. "We'll let you get back to the Double C early enough to get plenty of rest . . . and all those other things that newlyweds do."

Ruth nodded and Tyler grinned. "Champagne?"

"The best we have to offer," Scott assured them.

Tracey was about to excuse herself and prepare the nightly deposit, when Serena insisted she go along. "I couldn't," Tracey protested. "These people are your family. I'd just be an outsider in a private celebration."

"Don't be ridiculous," Beverly said.

"Everyone is family around here," Valerie said.

"That's right," Tyler added.

Faced with the encouragement of them all there, Tracey relented. It took a few minutes to get the store ready to close, but everyone waited patiently, then migrated en masse to the lounge.

Beverly and Tracey sat together, the only two without partners. "I wish Jeff was here," Beverly said with a sigh. "I thought everything would quiet down once the well came in, but now we have a whole new set of problems. As much as I miss him,

it's so important to him...to us... I can't be-
grudge him a minute that he has to spend there.''

Cal strode to the stage and took the microphone
that had been set up for the weekend's band. He
adjusted the controls to get rid of the feedback.
Then he called for everyone's attention.

"I have an important announcement.''

All eyes turned toward him.

"It's with great honor that I announce the marriage of my brother, Tyler McKinney, to a very
lovely lady, Ruth Holden.''

Though there weren't many people in the bar yet,
a huge cheer spread though the crowd.

"Drinks on me,'' Cal added.

Another even more enthusiastic roar accompanied the words.

The bartender began rushing around, refilling
drink orders. Scott disappeared into the back room,
then returned to the table, carrying a couple of
bottles of vintage champagne, followed by a waitress with a trayful of fluted glasses.

When everyone had drinks, Cal proposed a toast.
"May you find the same happiness with your lady
that I've found with mine.'' He wrapped his arm
around Serena's shoulders and pulled her against
his side.

"Thanks,'' Tyler said.

"May God bless you both, and keep you in the palm of His hand," Scott offered as a second toast.

"Here, here," they all agreed.

Glasses tinkled as their rims met, and everyone laughed as they shared the joy of the moment.

The festivities were still going strong when Manny arrived. As he hesitated in the doorway, Tracey felt her heart begin to skitter in her chest. She couldn't believe the way she reacted to his presence. It was like a light had been turned on in an underground cave.

"I think he likes you," Beverly whispered.

"Who? Manny?"

"Of course, Manny," Beverly said. "Did you notice the way he looked at you?"

"Manny and I are just friends," she protested.

Beverly winked. "Okay."

"I mean it."

"You can't tell me you're only friends, not with that expression on his face." Beverly smiled at Tracey. "Or the expression on yours."

Tracey hazarded a glance in his direction. He grinned and waved at her, but there was nothing else, nothing that should have made Beverly see anything out of the ordinary. "Just friends," she repeated. "I think he feels comfortable with me."

"That's a start, much better than the fireworks that threatened to explode every time I bumped into

Jeff. That we ever learned to even like each other is amazing. But you can't fool me. I'm in love and I recognize that expression on anyone's face."

Manny's boots echoed off the hardwood floor as he strode over to the corner where the group was gathered. Dressed in a simple faded blue chambray shirt and old jeans, he should have looked casual, even sloppy. But Manny carried himself proudly, his shoulders back and his head held high. With the first two buttons of the shirt open, revealing that sensuous swirl of dark hair, and the jeans just tight enough to mold themselves to his muscular thighs and tight buns, he was, in Tracey's opinion, the sexiest man in the room. Perhaps even the world. In spite of her protests, she realized she couldn't keep her eyes off him.

"Everyone needs a friend," Beverly continued. "And it's so much nicer if that friend is of the opposite sex."

Tracey swallowed a gulp of her champagne.

"Oh, oh. Don't look now, but he's headed your way. And he's got that look in his eye."

CHAPTER SEVEN

SHE WAS A SIGHT for sore eyes, Manny thought. Yep, a real sight.

Tracey seemed to be giving an extraordinary amount of attention to the glass of champagne in front of her. Her head was slightly bent and her hair fell across her face, shading her expressive eyes from him.

Evidently feeling his gaze, she looked up. And in her face, he read an expression he'd never seen there before. Was it possible she returned some of the feelings he was beginning to acknowledge?

He started toward her, noticing the way her fingers curled more tightly around the stem of her glass. Remembering his earlier thoughts about those fingers, his body reacted, swelling against the buttons of his jeans.

"Hey, Manny." Tyler held up a hand. "How 'bout joining us for a drink?"

"What's the occasion?"

"Ruth finally made an honest man out of Tyler," Scott supplied.

"Well, congratulations to you both," Manny said, shaking Tyler's hand.

"Thanks, Manny. By the way, I heard you did a great job patching up that horse of Carolyn's over at the Circle T. Hadn't been in town an hour before Dad was telling me the tales."

"He did," Beverly supplied from her end of the table. She nearly had to shout to be heard. "Mother has nothing but praise for Manny. She didn't think the horse would make it."

Manny caught Tracey's gaze on him. Their stares met, locked. Then she turned away.

"So, how about that drink?" Cal invited.

"Sorry, I can't. Still on duty. I just came to let Scott know I'm here and ready to start the checkups."

Scott nodded. "I'll come up to the stable with you. Just give me a minute, will ya?"

"No problem. Let me know when you're ready." Manny strode to the end of the table. "Hi, Tracey. Just thought I'd let you know how Sweetie's doing."

"Sweetie?" Beverly asked.

"Long story," Manny and Tracey said simultaneously. All three laughed. Tracey's laugh was clear and unpretentious, in the same way she was.

"So how is she?"

"Doing a lot better. She's getting around the barn on all four legs."

"Ready?" Scott called.

"Be right there," Manny answered, then addressed Tracey again. "Won't be much longer before we can turn her loose."

"I'm pleased to hear that."

"What have you got going on tomorrow?" he asked impulsively, then wondered where the offer had come from. He would be tied up all day with Scott and his animals. But it suddenly became important that he see Tracey, even if it was for only an hour.

"Working."

"Until what time?"

"Probably until one or so."

"How would you like to have lunch and see Sweetie?"

"I'd like that."

"Shall I pick you up at your place or the shop?"

"The shop," she answered.

"See you then."

All through the long evening, as he examined horse after horse and administered dozens of shots, thoughts of Tracey were never far from Manny's mind. It just wasn't like him. No, it wasn't like him at all.

"SO WHEN ARE YOU GOING to let her go?"

"Within a week or so," Manny said. "She'll become too dependent if we keep her much longer."

Tracey nodded, still stroking the length of Sweetie's neck. "She's really something."

When he didn't answer, she looked in his direction, surprised at the odd, speculative glint in his eyes.

"Ready for lunch?" he asked, changing the subject.

"Starving," she admitted. "I haven't had a decent meal all week and I'm too tired to cook when I get home from work."

"Good thing I cashed a check today," he said.

"Good thing," she agreed, laughing along with him. Again, she was struck by how comfortable the relationship with Manny was. She said goodbye to the deer, then joined Manny outside.

"I hope the Longhorn's okay with you," Manny said. "I have a prescription I need to drop off to a client. Since he couldn't make it during office hours, I promised to take it to him."

"Sure," she said.

During the short drive, he filled her in on what had happened since they last saw each other. The windows were open, to take advantage of the hint of refreshing fall crispness in the air.

The Longhorn Coffee Shop was doing a brisk business when they arrived. While Tracey secured a table for them, Manny met with his client. She was still studying the menu when he returned.

"Say, Manny, did you hear about Bubba?" Nora asked, coming over with an order pad.

"About his llama dying last week? That's the damnedest thing.... I'd have sworn that llama was healthy. I did an autopsy, but I couldn't find a single thing wrong with her." He shook his head, clearly puzzled by the unexplained death.

"No, about his horses. According to Mary, he's gonna buy himself another one. Looks like he's planning to go into business in a big way."

"It can be a good business," Manny said. "There's definitely money to be made with the right horses, good management and a lot of luck. No sense letting Florida and Kentucky grab all the horse racing glory."

Nora glanced around, making certain everyone was engrossed in conversations before continuing. "Mary talked to me about a job last week."

"Mary?" Manny asked. "She must be really worried."

Nora nodded. "She is. And I'm worried about her."

"I can see why."

"I promised Mary I'd talk to you. Bubba respects your opinion, and if you tell him a horse is too much and recommend he doesn't buy it, he'll listen to you."

"I doubt it," Manny replied. "He has definite ideas about getting into the quarter horse business, and he pays me to give him a medical opinion, not a financial one." He frowned. "Believe me, I already found that out. I recommended he not buy the first one. I'm surprised he hasn't told me about the second one, though."

Nora's face fell.

"I'm sorry, Nora. I'll do what I can, but don't expect it to be much."

"I knew you'd try," she said. "That's all I can ask for. Thanks."

Nora took their orders, then said, "Speaking of Bubba..."

The door slammed shut and Bubba strode over to them.

"Hey, Manny." He inclined his head toward Tracey. "Tracey."

"Afternoon, Bubba," Manny and Tracey answered simultaneously.

"Found me another horse, down near Corpus Christi. Looks great to me, but of course I'll be wantin' your expert opinion before I sign over the check."

"Sure, Bubba."

"How 'bout next weekend? I can wait till then, but the owner ain't gonna hold him much longer than that."

"Fine," he agreed, wanting to say something to the man, but not thinking this was the most appropriate time. "Give me a call at the office Monday and we'll schedule a time."

"Sure 'nough."

Neither Manny nor Tracey said anything until Bubba was well out of earshot.

"What are you going to do?" Tracey asked.

"Damned if I know." He stirred a packet of sugar into the cup of coffee Nora had wordlessly refilled. He shook his head and repeated, "Damned if I know."

After they left the Longhorn and were away from the many listening ears, Manny told Tracey about the quarter horse Bubba bought in Austin.

"Maybe I should have been more forceful when I suggested he shouldn't buy the animal."

"But you said yourself that it's not your place to give financial advice, just a medical opinion."

"The horse was sound," Manny said. "But the price was probably ten thousand higher than I'd expect to pay. Admittedly, the bloodlines were excellent, but..."

Manny's voice trailed off, and he shrugged as if he couldn't quite figure it all out. "I think he got all hung up on the fact the horse's name was Flying Wind and the name of his ranch is Flying Horse. He convinced himself it was a good omen."

"Maybe it'll work out," Tracey said optimistically.

"I hope you're right." He cut her a glance out of the corner of his eye. "Because I'd hate to see Mary hurt any more than she's already been."

Manny dropped Tracey off at her apartment with the promise that he'd stop by later if he finished at a decent hour. She tried not to count on it, but she caught herself glancing at the clock every thirty minutes all evening. When the doorbell finally rang around ten o'clock, she tried not to look as relieved as she felt when she opened the door and saw Manny standing there.

"Well, hi," she said with what she hoped was a casual flair. "Come on in. You're just in time for the news."

"Whew...I'm beat." He took off his Stetson and hung it on the brass coatrack near the front door. "We stopped for a quick dinner around seven, but I sure am thirsty. Do you want to go out for a drink?"

He looked so tired, and she was so glad he'd made the extra effort to stop by, that she couldn't bear the thought of making him leave again. "I have Corona," she offered.

"You remembered." He seemed genuinely touched by her thoughtfulness.

When she'd stopped by the store for a bottle of wine last night, she hadn't actually made a conscious decision to buy the six-pack, yet it had somehow ended up in her refrigerator...just in case. She even had a fresh lime to go with it.

He walked into the small kitchen area, which consisted of little more than a compact gas stove with a couple of burners, a small refrigerator, microwave and coffee pot. The area was made smaller by his overwhelming presence.

"Here, let me get that for you," he said, taking the bottle of wine and corkscrew.

While he poured her wine, she poured his Corona.

"Do you like old movies?" he asked.

"I love them," she admitted. What she didn't add was that she sometimes stayed up half the night watching them, snuggled under a blanket, with only a box of tissues for company.

"I've got a few videotapes over there in the bookcase," she said, hoping he would want to stay for a while.

"Sounds good to me." He gave her a teasing grin. "Trust me to pick one out?"

"Sure. Trust me to pop some microwave popcorn?"

"If I see smoke billowing from the kitchen, I'll call the fire department, then rush to your rescue."

"My hero," she said. "Save the building, then the damsel."

They shared another laugh, something she hadn't done with a man for a long time. But with Manny, it seemed natural.

A few minutes later, she walked into the living room and found him standing in front of the television set, a videotape in his hand.

"What did you pick?" she asked, not being able to read the title.

"It's a surprise."

He slid a tape into the VCR, and she set a bowl of perfectly popped kernels on the coffee table.

"Not even a scorched piece," he commented, examining the bowl with exaggerated concern.

"Must be the night for miracles."

They sat together on the couch, close but not too close. And not nearly close enough for Tracey.

The credits began to roll. *Casablanca.*

A guaranteed three-tissue movie.

"Do you approve?" Manny asked.

"It's probably my all-time favorite." She'd watched the movie once a year for the past ten or so years, and no matter how well she knew the ending and was prepared for it, she couldn't keep from crying.

She tossed a few kernels into her mouth, and watched as he did the same. As the love affair unfolded on screen, she had difficulty, for the first time, concentrating on the story. She was very much aware of Manny's presence, of his potent masculinity, his blatant sexual virility. And of her need.

Close to the end of the movie, she excused herself to go and blow her nose—and miss the part that usually reminded her of how the story would end.

But Manny had paused the tape. Good thing she'd unobtrusively wadded a handful of tissue and tucked it in her pocket.

No matter how hard she tried, she couldn't stop the knot from swelling in her throat. Or the tears from forming in her eyes.

"Not one of those sentimental types, are you?" Manny asked, looking at her.

"'Fraid so," she admitted, dabbing the corner of her eyes.

He moved closer, placing his arm around her. "Everyone needs a shoulder to cry on," he said.

She snuggled against him. His scent, which had only tantalized her from afar, now filled her senses. His arm tightened around her comfortingly and she relaxed against his side.

She glanced up at him and found his gaze was focused not on the screen, but on her. There was desire glowing in those onyx eyes, but there was also a hesitation, a confusion as if he didn't know quite what to do with her.

They both looked away, trying to concentrate on the movie and not on the possibility that this friendship could, very easily, become an affair. That was exactly the sort of relationship neither of them was looking for at the moment.

Manny stood when the closing credits scrolled across the screen. "Not bad," he said.

"Bogey's finest hour," she said.

"I don't know about that. I thought he was great in *The African Queen.*"

While they cleaned up the popcorn that had fallen on the floor, they shared an animated debate about movie roles and characters.

"Want a refill on your wine?" he asked, carrying the empty bowl into the kitchen.

"Sure," she said. "Just let me just check my mascara."

"Only your right eye is smudged."

"So gentlemanly of you to point it out," she said, strolling into the kitchenette and wiping her eye with an unused tissue.

"Hey, if I wasn't so much of a gentleman, I would have pointed it out earlier, while you were crying."

"I didn't cry," she protested.

"Did too," he countered.

She didn't argue. She'd been caught crying, and he hadn't vanished. "Okay, so maybe a tear or two."

"Or a bucket load."

"Or a bucket load," she conceded.

He popped the cap off another Corona. "But who's counting?"

"Obviously not you."

Manny held her glass of wine. She reached for it, having to move closer to him. Her heart rate increased and her breath seemed constricted in her lungs.

One thing was certain: no man had ever affected her the way Manny did...not even James, and she'd thought she loved him.

A knock on the door interrupted the growing intimacy. Tracey glanced at the clock on the microwave. Even though it was set ten minutes fast, it was still after midnight.

"Expecting company?"

"No," she replied. "Maybe it's Serena or Señora Sanchez."

"Do you want me to answer it?"

The knock sounded again. "I'll get it," she said. Manny nodded.

Tracey headed toward the door, conscious of Manny following, not far behind her. If there was any trouble, he'd be there. She found the thought comforting.

"Tracey, honey! Are you home?"

"Oh, God," she said with a groan.

"Trace?" he asked.

"It's my mother."

"Is that a problem?"

"You haven't met my mother."

Tracey pasted what she hoped was a warm, welcoming expression on her face, then went to answer the door. "Hi, Mother. Daddy."

"Tracey, darling," Donna said, capturing her daughter's face between her palms and bestowing a motherly kiss on her forehead. "We tried to call earlier and there was no answer. Daddy and I thought we'd stop by and make sure you were all right."

"Good Lord, Mother, it's the middle of the night."

"I know, dear. We got a late start."

She released her hold and Tracey stepped back a little. "Mother and Daddy, I'd like to introduce you to Manny Hernandez . . . a friend of mine." Tracey smiled, and held the door wide, inviting her parents in.

Her father kissed her on the cheek, then pulled away when he saw Manny.

"Oh," Donna said, "I didn't realize you had company, honey."

Manny walked over to them, a warm smile on his handsome face. "Mr. and Mrs. Cotter, pleased to make your acquaintance." He extended his hand to Tracey's father...who pointedly ignored the gesture.

Manny dropped his hand.

"A glass of wine, Mother? Corona, Daddy?"

"I only drink domestic beer, Tracey," her father said, his tone reproachful.

"And I don't imbibe, honey, you know that."

"I'll brew coffee," Tracey said, escaping to the kitchenette and feeling guilty for abandoning Manny. Her mother followed her.

"Honey, how long have you been seeing that *man?*"

"Manny? We're not seeing each other, exactly." Why was she hesitant to admit anything about her friendship with Manny to her mother?

"Well, what, *exactly?*"

"We've had dinner a couple of times." Tracey filled the filter with coffee, poured a pot of water in the top, then switched on the pot. She relaxed against the counter, arms folded in front of her chest. "There's nothing more to it, honestly."

Donna fanned herself. "I'm glad to hear that, honey." She darted a glance into the front room. "So it's not serious?"

Tracey smothered a groan. In spades, she remembered why she'd moved away from home. "It's not serious."

"Well, I'm glad to hear that."

The relief in her mother's tone was so insulting to Manny that Tracey felt compelled to defend their relationship, whatever it might be. "At least it's not yet."

"Tracey! What in heaven's name do you mean by that?"

"I mean I'm not ruling out the possibility."

Tracey moved around so she could see Manny and her father. Since she was a child, she'd been adept at reading her father's body language. She'd learned when to confess bad grades, when to brag about good ones. And she realized that at this moment, her father was as rigid as she'd ever seen him. That spelled trouble.

Desperate to get back in the living room and help relieve the tension she saw building, she hurriedly gathered coffee cups, sugar and cream.

"Honey, not to be rude or anything, but your Manny is—" her mother paused as if seeking the exact word, then finished with a horrified whisper "—Mexican."

"Really?" Tracey echoed. "Actually, he's American. He was born right here in Texas . . . just like me—just like you and Dad, too," she added for good measure.

Donna lowered her voice even more. "Honey, surely you can't—"

"Enough, Mother." Tracey slammed the drawer after taking out spoons.

Donna glanced at her only child with supreme surprise.

"I'm a grown woman, not your baby. Yes, Manny's of Mexican descent, but there's hardly a person in this country whose heritage didn't come from across a river or an ocean. Including ours."

"But honey, our family originally came from Ireland."

"And?"

"And?" Donna echoed.

"What's your point? That our skin color is different? Or our eyes?"

"Well—"

"Mother, stop. I won't allow you to criticize a man with whom I've chosen to associate." She laid the spoons on the tray where she'd already placed the cups and saucers. After taking a few deep breaths, she faced her mother again. "And I certainly won't allow your petty prejudices to ruin my friendship—and whatever else may develop in the future—with Manny." She grabbed up the tray, trying to stop her hands from shaking. "And that's final."

Donna sniffed. "I can't believe you spoke to me that way, Tracey Marie Cotter."

"Believe it," she said, leading the way from the kitchenette.

"Where's your respect for your mother, child? Why the Good Book says, 'honor—'"

"You know what I can't tolerate, Mother? Intolerance." She forced her voice to drop to a whisper, not wanting Manny to overhear it. "Prejudice is mean and nasty. And it's decidely unchristian. I will not tolerate it in my house."

"Why, I never—"

"You have now. You've demanded respect from me my whole life. Now I'm demanding it from you."

The atmosphere in the living room was taut with tension, much the same tension that hung between Tracey and her mother.

Tracey, pretending an oblivion she was nowhere close to feeling, placed the tray on the coffee table and said, "Manny played football for Texas A&M. He was a starter in the Cotton Bowl."

"That right?" Tom Cotter said.

Tracey sent a prayer of thanks heavenward. Her father was a big enough football fan to overlook Manny's heritage, at least for now.

While Tracey couldn't have called the next hour cordial, it was at least tolerable. She suspected her parents learned a lot about themselves, since they'd spent hardly any time ever in conversation with a living soul outside their strict Southern Baptist church denomination before.

When her parents left, heading for the nearest motel with promises to treat her to breakfast before they left the next day, Tom even offered his hand to Manny. It was a gesture she appreciated.

"Good night, Mother," she said, kissing her mother's cheek. "Thanks, Daddy." Tracey hugged her father.

"Well," Manny asked when she closed the door behind her parents, "did I pass inspection?"

"I'm sorry if they were rude, Manny. I would never have asked you to go through that."

"No apologies, Trace. It wasn't your fault. It actually wasn't a big deal to me," he assured her, closing the distance between them in a few, easy strides. "It's not the first time I've come up against racial prejudice in my life. Unfortunately, it won't be the last, either," he added softly, regretfully. Manny let his fingers tangle in the short length of her hair. "But I've learned to deal with it. It's one of the more unpleasant aspects of life as a minority. Luckily, though, most people look past it. People like you.''

Her knees felt weak.

''Your parents obviously love you, Trace. For your sake, if not mine, they're willing to tolerate me, even give me a chance.''

Tracey nodded. ''I think they actually like you.''

''How about you, Trace? You willing to give me a chance?''

He lowered his head toward her.

She looked up, helpless to resist, wanting his touch. Wanting to taste him. She licked her bottom lip.

''How about it, *querida?*''

''Yes, Manny.''

The last thing she saw before he claimed her lips was his soft, sensual grin.

But instead of the deep, passionate kiss her body ached for, he brushed his lips across hers in an almost brotherly fashion. However, she was relieved to notice that his hands were trembling as he grabbed her shoulders and pushed himself away.

''It's late and I'd better head home,'' he murmured, his voice husky.

She nodded, not trusting her own voice to not betray her feelings.

"YEAH, WE'LL BE DOWN sometime next weekend," Bubba said into the phone receiver. He listened to the person on the other end, somewhat impatiently.

"Look," he said not more than a minute later, interrupting the anxious voice, "I can't move too fast without raising suspicion. Just take it easy. We got away with the first one, now we've gotta play it cool. Besides, it'll take some time for me to round up all the money."

He cursed when he heard Mary's car pull into the driveway. "Look, I gotta go." He hung up without another word.

Bubba worked to shove away the metallic taste in his mouth.

"Evening, Al," Mary said, in that same singsong voice that used to wrap around him and squeeze at his heart.

"Mary," he said.

The phone rang again, and she started toward it. Bubba lunged, not wanting this moment to be spoiled by the sordid business he was involved with. "Hello?" Instantly recognizing the voice, he said savagely, "You got the wrong number." Then he slammed the receiver back into its cradle.

Mary. The ranch. Hell, he was on a one-way ticket to losing everything, unless this last bid worked out. In fact, he'd already started losing. On the quiet, his old friend J.T. had bought a share of the Flying Wind, agreeing to sell it back when—if—things improved.

They had to. After all, he had a reputation in Crystal Creek.

"You hungry, Al?"

"No, thanks, sugar. I ate in town a while ago."

She nodded. "Then how about a glass of iced tea?"

"That'd be nice," he agreed, watching her place her purse on the coatrack, then walk toward the kitchen. While she was gone, he took the opportunity to go into his office.

The envelope lay there on his desk, its white side slit open the moment the mail arrived that morning. Bubba reached inside and took out the check.

Fingering it, he felt slightly ill.

And yet it represented the only possible chance he, Mary—and the Flying Horse—had at survival.

CHAPTER EIGHT

MANNY FLIPPED through the files on his desk, making certain everything had been taken care of. He glanced through the billings, initialing them so Jennifer, his part-time receptionist, could mail them first thing in the morning.

The phone rang. He answered it on the first ring and heard Bubba's distinctive voice.

"Saturday afternoon is fine," Manny agreed. He took down directions and a phone number. "Great, I'll meet you out there."

The timing was perfect, Manny thought with satisfaction. He'd go down to Corpus Christi Friday night and visit his parents. He could head back Sunday. It was always a treat to combine business with pleasure.

Not a minute after hanging up with Bubba Gibson, Manny heard a knock on the glass pane of the front door. The street lamp reflected the golden highlights in his unexpected visitor's hair. Tracey.

"Trace," he said, turning the key in the lock. "Is everything okay?" She was the last person he expected, unless something had happened.

"I'm just so excited, I had to tell someone." She came in, tantalizing him with the faintest whiff of the cologne she sometimes dabbed on. "I was hoping you'd still be here. When I saw the pickup, I had to stop."

"I'm glad you did." He sat on the edge of the table, fascinated by how her eyes twinkled with animation. "Well?" he prompted.

"The store had its first five-thousand day."

"Five thousand? As in dollars?"

"As in dollars," she said breathlessly.

Tracey's breathlessness was honest, as refreshing as a Gulf breeze. "Congratulations."

"Serena wasn't home when I tried to call her and neither was Cal. You were the only other person I thought of to share the news with."

"I'm honored."

"Can you imagine?" she went on. "It's beyond our wildest dreams. In fact that's what it is, a dream come true. All the years we've sweated and labored together. Now we have the La Herencia Boot Stores. It's a reality and the success we've always wanted!"

"You're still sweating and laboring," he reminded her.

"Well, yes...but you know how it is when it's your own business," she said. "When something you always believed in happens. It makes all the hours, all the frustrations worthwhile."

"It does, indeed."

"This calls for a celebration," she said. "I'll buy you a drink at Zack's."

"Only if you let me buy dinner while we're there. If you had the kind of day you said, you probably only had half an apple for lunch."

"Half a banana," she corrected.

Then she smiled. Manny's insides melted quicker than a scoop of vanilla in the summer sun.

"It's a deal," she said.

"Just let me finish up my paperwork in the back and we'll be on our way."

"I'll go with you, if I won't be in the way."

"Sure, come on back. There's an extra chair."

In his office, he wished he hadn't issued the invitation. Tracey was a definite distraction. She didn't talk or bother him in any way, yet her presence was enough to make his mind wander into dangerous territory.

According to his reputation, he didn't hesitate to take what he wanted, but Manny hesitated with Tracey. More than once she'd hinted at an incident that had soured her on dating for several years. Serena had told him basically the same thing, before adding her warning—threat, Manny mentally amended.

Threats had never stopped Manny before. In fact, he'd taken a hell of a beating once, just to prove a threat didn't scare him. It was Tracey herself who stopped him. He didn't want to be the cause of the same sort of hurt he occasionally discerned in her eyes.

"I'm sorry," she said, capturing his gaze with the warmth of her amber-colored eyes. "I don't mean to rush you."

"You're not." No doubt about it, he couldn't work with her perched in his office. His hormones were in high overdrive. And inhaling her scent and seeing her perfect little rear perched on the desk in front of him only made it worse.

He slammed shut the file folder he was working on. He'd finish in the morning, even if he had to arrive half an hour earlier. With the way his body was responding, though, it would be a miracle if he got any sleep at all that night.

After closing the files and locking the drawer, he pocketed the keys. "Ready?" He flipped off the lights, then led the way into the reception area.

They spent an enjoyable evening together—except for the fact that his jeans felt uncomfortably tight and the food seemed completely tasteless. The only thing his mouth wanted to taste was Tracey's sweet lips and soft skin. After dinner, he drove her back to the clinic where they'd left her car.

Instead of climbing out and going around to open her door, he shut off the ignition and turned toward her. Only the glow from the street lamps and a sliver of moon lit the inside of the pickup. "Listen, Trace, I'm going to Corpus this weekend to check out that horse for Bubba and to see my parents. Why don't you come with me?"

"I don't know, Manny...."

Even in the dim light, he saw her fear. "No hidden agendas," he assured her. "I met your parents, I'd like for you to meet mine. We'll stay in a hotel Friday night. Separate rooms. Hell, separate hotels, if it'll make you feel better."

"Manny, I don't know what to say."

"Just think about it," he urged. "Don't turn me down flat without even considering it."

She smiled, a bit tentatively. "Okay," she agreed. "I'll think about it."

"AL, ARE YOU SURE we can afford it?"

"Not to worry, sugar, I've got it all worked out." Bubba threw an arm around Mary's shoulders. It seemed the harder he tried to hide the sordid details from her, the more she found out. And he didn't know how. Maybe it was her ability to interpret his moods after all these years.

"That horse in Corpus Christi is gonna be the answer to all our prayers, Mary," he said honestly. "She'll pay out big for us, sugar, I promise you."

"But where are you going to get the money to buy her?"

He sucked in a deep breath and answered, "Well, we got a check for our llama. Thank God for insurance. Wasn't much, but we weren't that short. Don't worry, Mary. Everything will work out."

She looked up at him.

"You do believe me, don't ya?"

"I believe you, Al."

He patted her cheek awkwardly, and avoided her eyes. Good God, but a conscience was a horrible thing, he thought as his wife responded with such sweetness and gentleness. If she ever found out what he'd done, she wouldn't be able to stand the sight of him.

Hell, at this point, he could hardly stand himself.

MANNY GLANCED OVER at the woman sleeping in the passenger seat. Slivers of silver light from the moon filtered through the tinted window, highlighting the glints in Tracey's hair.

He was glad she'd agreed to accompany him to Corpus Christi. He was getting serious about

Tracey, more serious than he'd ever been about a woman before.

He figured a weekend together was the perfect way for them both to explore their feelings. Manny wasn't a fool. He realized he and Tracey had some major cultural differences that would need to be worked around if something more permanent were to develop between them.

Whenever possible, he spent Sunday mornings at Mass in the Roman Catholic church. And he knew she regularly attended Southern Baptist services. She was as devoted to her religion as he was to his.

And Manny was doubly sensitive to the problem of their differing racial backgrounds. He'd dated a lot of Anglo women in his day, but often, when things got serious, even liberal people hesitated before crossing racial lines.

And it went both ways. His parents wouldn't be any more pleased that he was dating an Anglo than Tracey's parents had been to discover she had a man of Mexican heritage in her living room...in the middle of the night. He was sure they suspected the worst. Perhaps that was part of the reason he wasn't rushing things.

Family was important to Manny, just as he knew it was to Tracey. Could they handle all the obvious and unforeseen circumstances that would obstruct their relationship? Did they care enough to try?

One thing was certain. The weekend would be a test of their compatibility on several different levels.

Lights from the city ahead appeared through his windshield. He eased off the accelerator, dropping more to a city than freeway speed.

Tracey began to stir, making the soft sounds associated with being half-awake, half-asleep. Manny couldn't keep from wondering what she'd look like with her hair mussed from lovemaking, and her body flushed from his hands and his mouth.... His grip tightened on the steering wheel.

She rubbed her eyes with the back of her hand and yawned. "I can't believe I fell asleep."

"Kills my ego," he said. "I didn't realize I was so boring."

"You're not boring," she protested. "I'm just exhausted from putting in so many hours at the shop." She stretched. "It's exhilarating, but tiring," Tracey said, dropping her arms.

"We're almost at the hotel. I'll even tuck you in."

Except for the lyrical strum of George Strait's guitar strings in the cab, the only other sound was that of Tracey's shaky breathing.

"Look, Trace," he said. "Don't take what I said wrong. Nothing's going to happen this weekend that you don't want to happen. We're both grown-ups and we can deal with whatever might come along."

"I know."

Since his parents' place was so small, he'd called ahead for reservations at a hotel near their home, and within minutes they arrived at the hotel and secured the keys to their rooms.

"Why don't we stop at the bar for a drink before we turn in for the night?" he asked. "I'm a little strung out from the drive."

She agreed, so Manny gave the bellman a tip to take their luggage to their rooms while they strolled to the lounge. They found a quiet corner, away from the band, which was evidently on a break between sets. A waitress took their orders, then returned almost instantly, placing the drinks on the table.

Tracey told him of the week she'd had, about some of the more unusual orders and interesting people. "You should see the boots Beverly commissioned for Jeff. They're marvelous."

"Serena actually designed them with oil wells?"

"Yes, and there's oil spurting out of the top and even two people who, if you really use your imagination, look like Jeff and Hank. I think Beverly's really going to be pleased. We've got a photographer taking pictures of them to use in an advertising campaign we're launching next month."

"Sounds as though you're going to be busier than you already are."

Tracey twirled the glass stem between her fingers, looking at the wine as it slid back down the inside of the goblet. "The campaign's scheduled to go into three targeted markets with full-page ads in several selected newspapers and magazines. Four-color ads, if you can believe it. That's very ambitious for us."

Her animation and enthusiasm were contagious.

"Before Cal entered the picture, none of this would have been possible."

"I think it's a matter of teamwork, from what I've seen," Manny supplied.

"It is. Cal provided the backing, Serena the design and hand-tooling expertise, but I seem to have a knack for merchandising. And numbers." She wrinkled her nose. "Sometimes I wish I'd never let on about that."

Manny took a drink from the glass of cold cola he was holding. "Maybe you can give me a hand when my bookkeeper goes on vacation."

"Uncle!" she said with a laugh. "I've got enough paper to wade through at the shop. In fact, I've been doing most of the book work for the other store, too. We just don't seem to be able to keep help at that store. It looks as though I may have to start spending one day a week over there, as much as Serena and I hate for that to happen.''

"The joys of owning your own business,'' he sympathized.

"I wouldn't trade it for the world,'' she said. "But the better news is, Serena has come up with the prototypes for the line of holsters I designed, and I've been experimenting with styles of braiding and silver accents for the bridles.''

"I didn't know you were designing these days.''

"Neither did I,'' Tracey admitted. "But I came up with a few ideas and wanted to give them a try. Serena and Cal are both as excited about it as I am. Hopefully, we'll be able to start taking orders in the next few weeks.''

"I say this deserves a toast.'' He lifted his cola. "To Tracey and her success.''

Her goblet tinkled when it met the side of his glass, and their eyes sparkled in warm camaraderie across their drinks as they consummated their toast.

"Thanks.''

The band started to play again. The lead singer launched into his version of "The Thunder Rolls.''

"Shall we?'' Manny invited, offering his hand.

She smiled, accepting.

They shared wooden floor space with only two other couples. Manny pressed Tracey close against him, enjoying the feel of her, her softness and her sweetness.

"Sorry," she said, looking up after stepping on his toes.

"Don't worry, my fault." And it was, he knew. Instead of leading, he'd been content just to sway together in time to the music.

The song ended and they started to drift apart, until Tracey grabbed his hand and said, "Oh, I love 'The Dance.' It's one of my favorites."

"*Querida,* I'm happy to dance the night away with you, if that's what you want."

As he took her back in his arms and felt her cheek rest snugly against his shoulder, he wondered if dancing would be enough.

AS IT HAD TURNED OUT, dancing would have to be enough. It was obvious back in her room that Tracey was more skittish than the baby foals he brought into the world. If he'd pushed her into anything sexual, he sensed she would probably have regretted it.

And he would have regretted the knowledge he'd pushed and she'd succumbed. When he made love with Tracey, he wanted it to be because she wanted it as much as he.

So, he'd spent a restless night...all alone. The thoughts of her, lying half-naked on a bed in the adjoining room, was too much for his libido to bear. He kept thinking about how good her body felt snuggled against his and how soft she was in his arms and how warm she would be inside. . . .

"MORNING, MANNY," Tracey said, her voice unbearably perky for so early in the day. She'd just knocked and entered his room through the adjoining door, and she stood leaning against his dresser while he finished getting dressed.

"Sleep well?" he asked as he wiped the leftover streaks of shaving cream from his face.

"Yeah. You?"

He looked directly at her, capturing her gaze. "Like hell," he admitted honestly, pulling a fresh shirt from the hanger and shoving his arms in the sleeves. "One of the toughest nights I can ever remember."

She started to say something, but he interrupted.

"Are you ready to go?"

"Yes."

"Fine." Manny regretted his harsh tone, but he had to admit to being completely inexperienced when it came to this sort of thing. He'd never had a morning after without a night before. And he didn't know exactly how to act.

Within minutes, they were in the coffee shop, making inane conversation. Manny was grateful when Bubba arrived, a brand-new Stetson on his head. The man walked over to them, grinning as if he'd already raised a contender for the Breeders' Cup.

"Howdy, Manny. Tracey." If Bubba was surprised to see Tracey, he didn't show it.

"Join us for a cup of coffee before we head out?"

Bubba checked the oversize watch on his wrist. "I guess we got a couple of minutes before we have to drive on over to the appointment."

He grabbed a chair and pulled it up to the table. Manny signaled the waitress for another cup of coffee.

After she filled their cups, she left the bill. When the three were alone, Manny decided it was as good a time as any to honor his promise to Nora by saying something to Bubba about his new business.

Manny took a deep drink from the steaming coffee, then leaned back in his seat. "You know, Bubba, horse racing can be a real risky business. It can take big money, and you might never see a payoff."

Bubba nodded. "I got it under control." He stirred a third packet of sugar into his cup.

Manny and Tracey exchanged glances. "I'd just hate to see a situation where this was taking more of your resources than you were getting out of it."

"Thank you for your concern," Bubba said stiffly, clearly offended. He straightened his bolo tie.

Manny knew he'd touched a raw nerve. "Just trying to be helpful, Bubba."

"Well, like I said, much obliged for the concern. But I'll worry about my finances. You jus' stick to worrying about the health of my animals. No offense, if you know what I mean."

Manny nodded. "No offense taken, Bubba." He hadn't thought for a minute that Bubba would actually listen, but Manny always kept his word. And now he could tell Nora he'd tried.

"Shall we?" he asked, addressing Tracey and Bubba as he drained his coffee cup.

"Let me get that," Bubba said, picking up the check from the table. He dropped a substantial tip, then headed toward the cash register.

"That's not necessary," Manny said.

"I insist," Bubba said. "After all, you did make this trip on my account." That said, he pushed aside the back of his jacket and tugged his wallet from his tight pants pocket.

He smiled at the cashier, openly flirting with the young woman as he dropped a large bill on the counter.

Once again Manny and Tracey exchanged wordless looks, and once again, Manny was cognizant of being on the same wavelength as she was. By the expression on her face, he saw she was thinking the same thing he was—if Bubba was in such serious financial straits, why was he flashing fifty-dollar bills?

CHAPTER NINE

"WELL? WHAT do ya think?" Bubba asked.

Manny, on his knees in the soft dirt of the corral, ran a hand up the horse's flanks. "Well, he's young, strong and apparently in good health."

"Then I should buy him?" Bubba asked.

As he pushed to a standing position, Manny looked directly into Bubba's faded blue eyes. "Now, Bubba, I can't tell you whether or not to buy an animal...any animal. You wanted my opinion of his health. I gave it to you."

The horse's owner guffawed, then slapped Bubba on the back. "What did I tell you? That horse is an investment opportunity. Got you a deal here you cain't pass up."

Bubba rubbed his chin thoughtfully.

"Yes, sirree, Mr. Gibson. Got you the kind of horse you ain't never gonna see again at this price. Tell ya what, let's go talk a deal. Whad da ya say?"

Manny had heard basically the same spiel up in Austin. All owners had a deal that couldn't possibly be passed up. And he didn't have the stomach to listen to all the details again. Particularly when he had Tracey waiting for him. "Ready?" he asked her. She'd been leaning against the fender of the truck.

She nodded.

"Manny, thanks for making the trip," Bubba said as he pulled his checkbook out of his shirt pocket. "Much obliged. Bill me for your time on my monthly statement, hear? Tracey, nice to see ya again." Bubba tipped his hat, then turned to walk off with the other man. Back at the pickup whose red body was liberally dusted with a fine layer of dirt from the country roads, Manny helped Tracey in, holding the door for her.

"He seems pretty determined," Tracey noted as they pulled away.

"That's typical, from what I've seen. Bubba's jumping into the horse racing business with both feet." Manny checked the road for traffic, then accelerated. "And heaven help anyone who stands in his way."

TRACEY'S STOMACH KNOTTED with nervous tension as they pulled into the driveway of Manny's parents' home.

He shut off the engine, then turned to her. "My parents are from Mexico," he said. "They can be a little old-fashioned, maybe a bit overwhelming."

Tracey laughed, albeit nervously. "You survived my parents."

"So I did."

The front door to the tiny house was thrown open the second they started up the sidewalk. His mother rushed outside, an apron tied around her waist. Her hair, with strands of steel-gray threaded among the black, was braided and coiled on top of her head.

"Manny! *¡Hijo!*" she cried.

Manny hugged his mother, kissing her on the cheek. Tracey hung back and watched diffidently.

"*Madre,* I'd like to introduce my friend, Tracey Cotter. Tracey, *mi madre,* Lupe Hernandez."

"Pleased to meet you, Señora Hernandez," Tracey said, offering her hand.

The older woman accepted her hand, though her gaze remained on her son. Although she didn't mention it, by the time Señora Hernandez announced that dinner was ready, Tracey had come to realize that Manny obviously hadn't prepared his parents for the fact he was bringing home an Anglo woman. Señor and Señora Hernandez were unfailingly polite, but she caught the occasional strained glance between them.

Manny accompanied her to the dining room, his fingers resting lightly on the small of her back. She wondered about how proprietary the gesture looked to his parents.

They all sat at a small table covered with a white, Spanish lace cloth and set with fine china and elegant crystal goblets, evidently to welcome the guest Manny was going to bring home.

The dinner, a fresh salad, homemade tamales, beans and tortillas, was wonderful. The flan the *señora* served was gourmet, restaurant quality. But the atmosphere was something less than totally pleasant.

Tracey sipped from her wineglass, hoping to relax a little more. But it didn't help. Manny was clearly uncomfortable, and his feelings telegraphed to her, making her even more nervous.

Reminders of a culture and background very different from Tracey's own were evident throughout the house. A crucifix hung over the kitchen door. A statue of the Madonna, palms outstretched, dominated the buffet. A string of rosary beads was draped over the Madonna's head, the wooden orbs small and obviously well-used. Tracey had noticed a nearly dry container by the front door for holy water.

"So, you're leaving tomorrow morning?" Ramon Hernandez asked.

"Yes."

"Manny, Tracey can stay in your old room, and I'll make up the sofa for you," Lupe offered.

"Actually, we didn't want to crowd you, so we're staying at the hotel."

The silence was tense.

"I see," Lupe said eventually. She stood and began gathering dishes.

"Let me help," Tracey offered.

"No, you relax," Lupe said.

"I'll give my mother a hand," Manny said to Tracey softly.

She nodded.

Manny grabbed the plates, then followed his mother into the kitchen. Ramon stayed at the table with Tracey. Without any warning, he looked directly at her and asked in Spanish, "So how long have you been seeing my son?"

A test? she wondered. Easily, she responded in his native language. Ramon was obviously surprised...and impressed, lifting a single black brow in the same way Manny did. As they continued to talk, mostly on neutral topics, Ramon seemed to relax a little, even managing to smile once or twice.

A few minutes later Manny and his mother returned. Both were ominously quiet.

"You ready to go, Trace?"

She looked at him, then back to his mother. "If you are," she agreed, and followed him to the closet. "We don't need to leave on my account," she whispered. "I understand how it is with parents."

"Look, Tracey, I appreciate how magnanimous you're being, but if it's all the same to you, I'd like to get the hell out of here."

She accepted his help into her light jacket while wishing she could say or do something to ease the tension.

They said their goodbyes and Tracey noted a sheen of tears covering Lupe's eyes, but proudly, the woman tried to pretend nothing was wrong.

Outside, Tracey wrapped her hand around his upper arm, pulling him to a stop. "Manny, you can't do this. Your mother's hurting. Don't leave her now."

"Tracey, you don't understand."

"Manny, I do understand," she corrected. "Your parents care about you...you just can't walk away. Go back and make your peace. I'll wait in the truck." When he made no move, she said, "Go. Reassure your mother, Manny. The rest can be worked out."

"Tracey, your optimism is one of the things I like best about you." He looked at her, his dark eyes seeming to see through to her soul. "And it's one of your most infuriating traits."

"Because I'm right," she said softly.

"Yeah," Manny agreed. "Because you're right."

The understanding that passed between them was like a bolt of electricity from the storm that had brought them together.

"Come in with me. You don't need to wait in the truck."

"I'll wait outside. This is something between you and your parents. My being there might only make it worse."

"You sure?"

"I'm positive."

"I'll be right back," he promised, then raised her hand to his lips.

She watched the door close behind him. Never had she felt so much desire for a man. And never had he seemed farther out of her reach.

"I FEEL SICK," Mary confessed.

Nora looked at Mary sympathetically, reached for the coffeepot and poured two cups. After turning off the neon Open sign, she picked up the cups and slid into the booth across from Mary.

Nora sympathized only too well with the older woman. Before Ken entered her life, Nora had known the kind of problems with Gordon that Mary now faced. Yet Nora realized it might actually be worse for Mary because Mary obviously still loved her husband.

Despite his relationships with other women? Just yesterday, Bubba had been in the café with Billie Jo Dumont. Mary wasn't a stupid woman. Evidently, she chose just to look the other way when it came to her husband's infidelity.

And if that was the case, there was no cause to hurt and humiliate Mary further. And, goodness knew, she already had plenty to deal with.

"So what's the matter?" Nora asked.

"He called from Corpus Christi a little while ago."

"And?"

"And he's bought another horse."

Nora felt her own stomach twist in sympathy to Mary's problem. "Oh Lord!" Nora said.

Mary's fingers trembled as she held her cup.

"I spent the day in his office," Mary admitted, shamefaced.

"There's no reason to feel guilty," Nora insisted, covering Mary's hand with her own. "You have every right to know your financial situation."

"You really think so?"

"Absolutely," Nora insisted. "This is the nineties, hon. Marriages are a partnership, not a dictatorship."

Mary seemed to take confidence from Nora's firm statement. "All our credit cards are at the maximum," she confessed. "I guess he's been taking cash advances from them."

Nora winced.

"Cody Hendricks at the bank left a message on the answering machine for Al yesterday. He said it was really important and that they needed to schedule a meeting first thing Monday morning." Mary paused, taking another sip from the nearly empty coffee cup.

She leaned back against the vinyl booth and let out a weary sigh. "But the worst thing is that Al won't tell me how bad things are. He keeps saying we've had a temporary setback."

Nora waited patiently while Mary considered just how much to admit. Mary wasn't one who usually spilled her problems.

"I don't know, Nora. To me it looks like more than a temporary setback. There's very little money in the checking account and a pile of bills hidden in the bottom drawer. And he just keeps spending. Not hundreds, but thousands. Honestly, I don't know what to do."

"If you need a loan..."

An expression of pure horror chased across Mary's face, making Nora instantly regret her words. Mary was a proud woman. Talking about her problems had obviously been very difficult for her and taking money from a person who couldn't really spare it would be unthinkable. "I'm sorry," Nora said softly. "I was only trying to help."

"I know," Mary said, schooling her expression into the serene look Nora was accustomed to.

TRACEY PULLED the one dressy outfit she'd packed from the suitcase. Remembering that she'd left the bag with her high heels in the car, she knocked on the adjoining door. After hearing a muffled "come in," she opened the door, then stopped dead in her tracks.

Manny emerged from the bathroom, damp curls clinging to his forehead. A white towel, wrapped casually around his waist, only served to emphasize the darkness of his bronzed skin.

She had the sudden compulsion to touch him, to feel the strength of his muscles and the texture of the mat of black hair that curled on his chest and trailed down his stomach to disappear beneath the towel. She gulped.

His just-showered scent of soap and musky cologne filled her senses. She wanted him. Wanted to be in his arms, held against his chest.

"Uh...I need the truck keys," she managed to say.

His sensuous lips slid into a teasing grin. "No pockets," he said, glancing down at his almost nude body. "But you can search me if you want to."

Tracey's gaze automatically was drawn to the general area where his pants pockets should be, then she snapped her head back up. She knew her cheeks were pink as she turned away, walked to the dresser and picked up the keys that were lying there next to his wallet, a comb and a handful of change.

She retrieved her bag, then went to his room to return the keys. Manny was lounging against the doorjamb. Their eyes met...their gazes held...the electricity crackled across the narrow space.

She held her bag against her chest, then headed back to her room, firmly closing the door behind her.

She stepped beneath the warm spray to take a quick shower. After that, she spent longer than usual on her makeup. And thirty minutes later, dressed in a black silk sheath dress and tiny, strappy sandals, she knocked on his door again.

Manny called for her to come in, then, using the remote control, turned off the television and stood, appraising her. A grin sauntered across his face. And he whistled. Long, deep and sexy.

"You look beautiful, Trace," he said.

He said her name, dropping the *y*, and dragging the *s* sound for a sensual sizzle. A spark of recognition lit somewhere deep inside her. He desired her. And that knowledge was incredibly gratifying.

"Thanks." She returned the smile. "After a month of wearing nothing but jeans and boots, it's nice to dress up." Under his scrutiny, she actually felt beautiful, for the first time ever. "You look great, too."

While she'd been getting dressed, Manny had changed into a charcoal-gray suit, the dark color serving to emphasize the richness of his eyes and hair. A crisp white shirt and wine-red tie added a snazzy complement. She automatically glanced at his boots. They were new, shiny, but identical to the ones everyone else in town was wearing. A thought, planted by Beverly, began to formulate in Tracey's mind.

"Shall we?" he asked.

She grabbed a light sweater. He took it from her, holding the garment while she slipped into it. His fingers lingered a few seconds longer than necessary on her shoulders, but she didn't object.

He slid her a glance as he started the truck. His eyes, his scent, his touch all combined to make a powerful aphrodisiac. Even the light from the moon added a mysterious element. Tracey shivered.

"I can turn up the heater if you're cold," Manny said.

"No, I'm fine," she answered, knowing she wasn't really "fine" at all.

They arrived at the restaurant where he'd made reservations, and she was impressed by the upscale elegance.

Dinner passed in a blur for Tracey. Manny was completely solicitous, keeping her entertained and her champagne glass full. She had more to drink than usual, but neither cared nor wanted to stop.

They shared a dessert, and sometime between the first bite and the last, he removed his suit coat and hung it on the back of his chair.

"Dance?" he asked, when she placed her fork down on the empty plate.

"I'd love to."

He stood and extended his hand. Tracey placed her much smaller one in his palm and he folded his fingers around hers. Slowly, he drew her to him, adjusting his grip until their fingers were entwined. Her insides tightened with each step they took toward the dance floor.

To a sweetly romantic selection by a female vocalist, they swayed. Tracey nestled against his soft cotton shirt, conscious of the texture of his chest hair beneath the material, and of the beat of his heart.

Manny's fingers moved up her spine caressingly. They caught in the hair that she'd shaped into a vee at her nape, then moved higher, tangling in the strands. Tracey sighed from deep inside, wishing the dance would never end.

But all too soon, it did, and the singer slid into a more upbeat number that broke the mood.

"More champagne?" he whispered.

"Sure."

The waiter had cleared everything except the bottle and two glasses. He'd replaced the candle, so the light flickered with the movement of air, illuminating the depths of Manny's dark eyes. He topped up her glass, then handed it to her, brushing her fingers.

"You're a great dancer," she said, lifting the glass to her lips.

"So are you," he said. "You move very naturally with me."

"To be honest, I usually step on my partner's toes, as you already know." She sipped, letting the dryness of the wine tantalize her.

"Maybe we're just meant to be together."

She wondered if he intended a double entendre, or whether she was reading between the lines, hearing something she wanted to hear.

Manny poured the last of the champagne into their glasses and asked, "Should I order another bottle?"

"No. Not unless you want to carry me back to the hotel."

He quirked one brow. "That has intriguing possibilities."

A flush crept up her face. "How do you do that?" she asked, changing the subject.

"Do what?"

"That, with your eyebrow."

"What do I do with my eyebrow?"

"Arch it," she said, resting her chin on her fist. "But just one at a time."

"This?" He demonstrated.

"That," she said, stifling a giggle.

"I don't know. Can't everyone?"

She tried, and only succeeded in raising both her brows simultaneously. "No. I guess not."

The singer struck up an old eighties song, one about love and the pleasures of making love.

"Care for one last dance before going back?"

Back. The single word held a wealth of implications. "Are your toes up to it?"

"*Querida,* you haven't stepped on my feet once. Not even when you tried."

During the dance, she didn't step on his feet, but it was partially because of the intimate way he held her. They stood closer than toe to toe.

The only problem with dancing this close was that she couldn't see his face, couldn't read his expression to see if he was as affected as she by their intimacy. Not that other parts of his body weren't responding to her. With every step, his rigid masculinity pressed against her stomach, exciting her thoughts and making her heart perform acrobatics in her chest.

He held her until the final notes trailed off. Even then, she was reluctant to leave his arms. Hand in hand, they walked to the table. Without a word, he grabbed his suit jacket, then claimed her sweater at the door. Manny draped the material across her shoulders and placed his arm around her waist possessively as they left the restaurant.

At the truck, he held the door open for her, then leaned inside to surprise her with an all-too-brief kiss. He stepped back, shut her door and walked around to his side. But even before he got in, his cologne clung to the still-warm night air, holding a promise of passion.

In that moment, Tracey knew she wanted it all.

CHAPTER TEN

BUBBA LOOKED IN on Mary. The light from the hallway spilled through the door he'd opened a crack.

He stood there for a couple of minutes, getting accustomed to the dim light, as he watched the shallow rise and fall of her chest. She slept peacefully, her forehead devoid of the lines he'd become accustomed to seeing over the past few weeks. Her seeming serenity surprised him, considering their conversation earlier that evening.

She'd confessed her concern and fright over what their future held. And she'd mentioned the dreaded word... bankruptcy. The nasty taste of bile rose in his mouth now the same way it had earlier this evening.

They'd had a fight. A real doozer, which they hadn't experienced since the early days of their marriage. What particularly rankled about this argument was that Mary was right.

In the bed, she breathed a gentle sigh, then turned over, bringing him back to the present. Her hand fanned across the pillow on his side of the bed. Then he saw a half smile form on her features.

For a reason he couldn't have explained if he had wanted to, Bubba walked into the room, for now ignoring the pull toward the barn...and the light steadily illuminating the open space there.

A feeling of tenderness touched him. He stood near her, so close he caught a hint of the soap she'd used since the day he met her—could it have been thirty years ago already? Way back then he'd sworn to make her his bride and build the Flying Horse to greatness with her by his side.

And they had been successful for a long time. Nearly a quarter of a century. But, as it had so many others in the past few years, the economy hit the Gibsons and the Flying Horse hard. They'd had to sell most of their cattle and heavy equipment and mortgage everything to the hilt. Despite it all, his determination to provide for Mary had remained a constant—even if he did have to admit that he often found pleasure in other women. In Bubba's eyes, there was a big difference in the feelings he had for his wife and for the women he saw while in town. Mary was above them all. Way above.

He sighed deeply, wishing things had never gotten as bad as they had—wishing he'd never had to resort to deceit to save everything—wishing he had another choice than what he was about to do.

Bubba turned away and closed the bedroom door behind him. As he walked down the stairs, he hoped his courage wouldn't desert him.

But he had to do it tonight...tonight, while Manny was still in Corpus with Tracey. If Bubba's guess was right, it would be late tomorrow before the veterinarian would be back in Crystal Creek. Hell, if Bubba had Tracey with him, he wouldn't be in a hurry to get back to work, either.

He opened the front door. The night air, while still warm, held more than a little humidity. The cloying atmosphere only made things worse.

Bubba could not rid himself of the metallic taste that still clung to his tongue and his teeth. Still, the thought of what he stood to lose forced him on. He closed the weathered wooden door behind him and headed for the barn.

As he got closer and his eyes adjusted to night-vision, he saw that the truck was already parked where Bubba had instructed. From inside the barn, a horse whinnied.

Another flood of bitterness coated the inside of his mouth. He cursed, a curse only ranch hands used, and never in polite company.

Hell.

He didn't want to go through with this. But he didn't want to face bankruptcy, either. And no one had caught on when the llama died. Which didn't make it right, he knew—just possible.

He opened the heavy barn door, wincing at the loud creak that seemed to reverberate through the still, dead air, then pulled it shut behind him.

He was already there, standing outside Flying Wind's stall, stroking her beautiful chestnut head.

She looked so proud and graceful, so goddamn trustful. And so did the brand-new horse he'd just brought home earlier that evening. Hell, he hadn't even been able to find it in him to call the animal by name. Probably better, he thought.

This was sick, he knew. Even for him.

"About time," the other man said.

Bubba swore again, before spitting in the hay. Anything to rid himself of the vile taste of death.

MARY BECAME AWARE of Al's absence the second he left the bedroom. She fought through the dreamy layers of sleep, the one state in which she'd found comfort and security over the past few months.

In her dream, as in many of the others she'd been having during the past weeks, J. T. McKinney and his young bride Pauline had visited Mary and Al, filled with plans for the Double C.

The four of them had spent many evenings together, laughing, joking, making big plans for the future, certain they would revolutionize ranching in the Lone Star state. Back then, she hadn't thought it possible for life to get much better.

But how things had changed. Pauline was dead, and the children she and J.T. had brought into the world were now adults with lives of their own. And things had gone full circle when J.T. had recently fallen in love with and married Cynthia Page, a socialite from Boston. Much younger and beautiful, Cynthia had unintentionally made Mary feel all of her fifty-four years.

The ranches, too, had changed dramatically. The Double C was still holding its own, but the Flying Horse was dying a slow, painful death.

Mary forced her eyes open as the now-familiar feeling of panic swept through her once again. "Al?"

She didn't really expect an answer. Many nights she turned on the bedside lamp, only to discover Al was gone. And last night, he hadn't been home at all. He'd been in Corpus buying that second horse they couldn't afford, even with the loan consolidation Cody Hendricks at the bank had been kind enough to float them.

Slipping from beneath the quilt she'd lovingly pieced, Mary grabbed her full-length chenille robe

from the arm of a wing chair. She wrapped it
around her, then started down the stairs, her fingers lightly gripping the banister. Maybe Al was in
the kitchen or his office. Worrying. Though he
pretended to be strong and unconcerned, and dismissed her fears casually, she was sure he'd dropped
a few pounds in the past weeks.

Al's appetite—appetites, she mentally amended
with a private, pained sigh—didn't diminish unless
he was worried. The weight loss and his absence
from their bed that evening concerned her.

A ribbon of light showed from beneath the
closed door of his office. She knocked.

"Al?" she asked when, after a few seconds,
she'd received no reply. When she finally pushed
open the door, only the illuminated green-shaded
banker's lamp indicated the room had recently been
occupied.

Otherwise, the office appeared immaculate. For
most of the years of their marriage, Al's desk had
been a mess of strewn file folders, loose pieces of
paper and unbalanced bank statements. But now,
everything was carefully locked in a huge cabinet.

Closing the door again, she headed toward the
kitchen. That part of the house was dark. Still, she
continued in the direction of the large sliding glass
window, then pulled back the drapes and gazed out
into the thick darkness of night. The moon, play-

ing hide-and-seek with the clouds, spilled enough light for her to see the few hundred yards to the barn.

A truck, whose color she couldn't quite make out, stood near the door. Maybe it belonged to one of the ranch hands, she thought. Odd, though, that anyone should be there at this hour.

The barn door opened a crack and a man she'd never seen before emerged, grabbing something from the bed of the truck. For an indecisive moment, she stood there, debating her options.

She didn't know where Al was or if the stranger meant harm. Instinctively, she eyed the locked gun cabinet, and the shotgun that showed through the glass etched with ducks and deer. The sight of the long-barreled gun comforted her. She hated to shoot, but knew how, and would if she had to.

When the man returned to the barn, he pulled the door wide. Al was standing just inside, and he didn't appear to be in any trouble.

Mary dropped the drape abruptly, and whirled back toward the stairs. From deep within had come a warning that she didn't really want to know what Al was up to in the barn at midnight.

She climbed back into bed and closed her eyes, but this time sleep was not so kind.

BACK IN Manny's hotel room, Tracey self-consciously fluffed her short hair while Manny released the knot in his tie. Within seconds, the loose ends of silk hung down his snowy-white shirt.

Momentarily, she turned to face him, her hips casually resting on the dresser. Manny shrugged from his suit jacket, folded it carefully, and placed it on the chair next to the bed. Then, surprisingly, he sat on the bed, leaned back against the headboard and folded his arms across his chest, pulling the material of his shirt taut. "Tracey," he began quietly, "tell me you want to make love with me tonight. Tell me I haven't misinterpreted anything."

Manny wasn't leaving her any room for regrets, for second thoughts. He was demanding the same honesty from her that he demanded from himself. If she said no, he would accept her decision. Of that she had little doubt.

"Yes, Manny," she whispered, barely able to squeeze the words out through the conflicting feelings of anticipation and fear zinging through her. "I want you. I want you to make love to me."

"Oh, Trace."

His voice sounded incredibly tight, husky. It sent a hot shot of longing all the way down to her toes.

And then she was in his arms, nestling her body into a perfect fit between his legs. She was beyond thinking, beyond wanting anything but to be with Manny.

She looked up at him as he pushed her bangs back from her eyes. He captured her chin between his fingers, gently holding her for his kiss. When it came, the sensation was sweeter than she'd imagined.

His lips found hers, soft and coaxing at first, then more demanding and enticing as he deepened the kiss, and opened her mouth. The touch of the tip of his tongue to hers—moist against moist, heat against heat—caused a ripple of pleasure to chase through her, settling somewhere in the pit of her stomach.

She felt his palm on the small of her back, the other hand at her nape. He held her so securely, as if he never wanted to let her go.

His intensity emboldened Tracey. She reached around his neck to finger the rich thickness of his hair.

The kiss lasted forever—forever and not nearly long enough.

Finally, Manny held her away from him and looked at her, communicating to the depths of her soul with his eyes. Then, without a word, he swept her into his arms. Tracey's breaths came in short, unequal gasps, and yet she wanted this—him— more than anything.

With an assertiveness foreign to her, Tracey reached for the dangling ends of his tie. She pulled Manny toward her, rewarded when she recognized the spark of excitement lighting his expression.

The vibrant sound of his laughter reverberated against her ear as she pulled him even closer. At last, she released one end of the tie, then slipped it from around his neck, and dropped it to the carpeting while she switched her attention to the top button of his starched shirt. He gulped as her knuckle brushed his Adam's apple, and she watched the movement along his tanned neck with fascination.

"Trace." Her name emerged from him raggedly.

She tried for a little finesse, but her fingers shook too badly. Each button that surrendered offered her a better view of his broad chest and the flat plane of stomach. Nothing in her experience could have possibly prepared her for the sensations building inside her.

Before reaching the last button, she pulled the shirttails from his pants.

"Man," he said quietly, "this is torture, Trace. As much as I want you to touch me, you're driving me crazy."

He stood, wrestled with the final button, then tugged his arms from the sleeves.

Tracey's breath froze. The mat of hair covering his chest was incredibly provocative. Her fingers ached to bury themselves in the ebony curls. Muscles bulged in his upper arms and the color of his skin was like molten honey burned by the summer sun. He was the sexiest man she had ever seen.

Manny fumbled with his belt, but never slid the leather from its nesting place. With his eyes on Tracey, he started to lower the zipper, cursing softly in his native tongue. At last, he shucked off the summer blend of wool, letting the pants drop to the floor to reveal bright red underwear.

"Aren't you going to finish undressing?" she asked, feeling unusually brave.

He did.

Tracey swallowed, her gaze irresistibly drawn to the swollen evidence of his desire. She longed to touch him, to taste him, to feel him deep inside her, but when he joined her on the bed and reached for her, nervousness and excitement warred within her. "I'm not very good at this," she admitted.

"Shh."

The word was barely a whisper, unfurling comfort through her mind. She'd seen Manny at his soothing best before, and knew she could trust him with her secrets.

"My only sexual experience was a disaster."

Manny captured her chin in his long fingers and turned her back to face him. "Then I'll do my best to make sure this time isn't, *mi querida.*"

He leaned closer, brushing her lips gently with his. He didn't push her any further, just encouraged her to give what she wanted. When he fumbled with the belt at her waist, she helped him, desperate for them to accomplish the task quickly.

Next, he concentrated briefly on her dress. He slowly eased the zipper down her back, and when the fabric yielded, he brushed it off her shoulder, kissing her naked skin as the garment slipped down her arms. A dart of desire arced through her, dancing along her nerve endings as his tongue left warm, wet trails.

"I'd never have figured you as the type to wear a teddy," he whispered, his breath tickling her ear. Even that sensation was new, tantalizing.

"I'm not. At least I wasn't until this trip."

"Is it too much to hope you were thinking of me when you packed it?"

He pushed one of the thin straps off her shoulder, and she trembled as his fingertips followed the lace all the way down. "I was thinking of you," she admitted softly.

He was completely hypnotizing. Under his spell, she felt she was the only woman in the world, the only person who mattered.

She enjoyed his gentle touch as he lowered the other strap. But instead of proceeding to take the material all the way off, he laid her back onto the mattress.

When he positioned himself over her, she noticed a telltale pulse in his temple.

"Having you undress me was agony," he admitted. "Having patience with your clothing is torture." He stroked her neck with the back of his hand, dragging his fingernails across her sensitized skin.

He'd barely touched her, yet she was more ready than she'd ever been. She arched her back, asking for more. But he was slow to give it.

By aching measures, he started to shimmy the teddy down. She lifted her hips, trying to encourage him along, but he would have none of it. With his palm, he pushed her back onto the bed, then continued his stroking, lazy appraisal of her.

"Not yet, *querida*," he said. "Not yet."

He bared her breasts, and her nipples instantly contracted into tight nubs. She groaned. She wanted him, needed him. "Manny..."

With one hand, he cupped a breast, letting it fill his palm.

"You're beautiful, Tracey. Perfect."

If he didn't touch her, she'd go mad. Manny insinuated himself between her legs, but she felt none of the stirrings of panic that she'd experienced previously. Manny inspired her complete trust. She knew he wouldn't hurt her.

When his lips closed around one of her painfully tight nipples, his mouth, teeth and tongue brought her to a height she'd never known existed. And yet simultaneously, he encouraged a need for more. Passion was stoked deep inside, and she knew she was close, very close.

He found her other nipple, rolling it between the thumb and forefinger of his free hand. While his tongue laved away the exquisite hurt from her other breast, he slipped his hands inside her teddy and started to lower it.

Briefly, he rolled off her in order to finish removing the teddy and to grab the condom from his wallet. Her body throbbed anxiously in the few seconds he was gone.

But Manny quickly returned to her, bombarding her senses once again with his expert touch and infinite patience. Feeling selfish, she tried to return some of the attention.

"Later," he promised. "This time is for you, Tracey." He smiled and her heart tripped. "Later is for both of us."

Her fingers caught in his hair as he returned, caressing her thighs, gently moving his hands along her tender skin. His touch was so close to her aching femininity, yet so far away. "Manny!" she moaned.

Wildly, she started moving her hips against his hand. When he placed a kiss on the top of her forehead, he distracted her momentarily and she opened her eyes.

He slipped inside then, and she gasped. Within seconds, though, the tiny pain receded.

"Okay?"

"Fine," she said.

Only then did he begin to move. She matched her motions to his strokes, feeling every heartbeat, watching his intense expression as he climbed with her toward a climax.

A wonderful relaxation, unlike anything she'd ever felt, washed over her. She shuddered, clinging to Manny and calling his name. Unbelievably, the satisfaction increased as she felt him join her, taking on his own pleasure.

They lay together for a long time, both exhausted.

"Am I hurting you?" he asked.

She heard his still-labored breathing, and wanted to prolong the feeling of being cherished a little while longer. "No."

"I'll move."

Tracey wrapped her arms around him, and continued to run her fingers across his back. "You're fine."

So, he held her closer, fitting their bodies together. A few minutes later, she heard his breathing slow considerably, and she knew he'd fallen asleep. Unconsciously, his arm tightened across her middle, as if he'd never let her go.

THE PHONE RANG, shattering the peace of the night. "Damn," Manny said, groping for the receiver in the unfamiliar surroundings. He squinted at the digital numbers on the clock. Three a.m.

The obnoxious sound shot through his head again, echoing. "All right, all right," he muttered. He continued to grope with his right arm, since the left was securely pinned beneath Tracey's back.

On the third ring, he managed to grab the receiver and bring it to his ear. Closing his eyes again, Manny muttered what he hoped was an appropriate greeting—and not what he really wanted to say.

"Phone's ringing," Tracey murmured, more than a bit belatedly.

"Got it, *querida*," he said, before trying to concentrate on his caller.

It took Manny a good twenty seconds to make sense of what was being said...and by whom.

"Bubba? What's the matter, buddy? It's the middle of the night."

A few of Bubba's hysterical words finally penetrated Manny's sensually sated mind. Exhaustion fell away in waves. In its place, nervous adrenaline swept through him. "Whoa," Manny said. "Slow down."

Tracey sat up, the sheet falling away from her bare breasts. Manny forced himself to assimilate what Bubba was saying. "The new horse?" he repeated.

"Dead!" Bubba yelled, his voice blasting through the phone.

Manny's face drained of color. Holding the receiver away from his ear for a second, he wiped his face with his hand.

"Manny!"

"I'm here, Bubba. Are you trying to tell me the new horse is dead?"

"Manny?" Tracey asked, her voice full of concern. "What is it? What's the matter?"

"Yeah, Bubba. I'm listening. Right. I'll be there as soon as I can."

He hung up, stunned. First the llama, then the new horse. Two deaths on a ranch whose animals were his responsibility. Hell.

"Is everything okay?" she whispered.

Manny turned on the light, then shook his head. "The horse we looked at this morning is dead."

"Dead?" Tracey echoed, her voice mirroring his own shock. "But he looked fine."

"Yeah, I know." Manny searched his mind for an answer, anything to give him a clue as to what might have happened, but found nothing. "Bubba said he couldn't sleep so he went down to the stables. The horse was lying in his stall." He dragged his fingers through his hair. "It just doesn't make sense. That horse was healthy. But then, so was the llama. I can't figure out..."

Before he finished the sentence, he'd climbed out of bed and grabbed his suitcase from the closet. He tossed it on the bed and grabbed a fresh pair of jeans.

He felt the reassuring touch of Tracey's fingers on his arm before she, too, got up.

She dressed and packed without comment, and within minutes, he'd turned in the keys to the night drop box and helped Tracey into the pickup.

A couple of hours later, the sun dawned bright and bloodred. He hardly noticed, nor was he really cognizant of Tracey dozing next to him. All the way back to Crystal Creek, the word *dead* repeated itself in his mind.

Dead...dead...dead...

CHAPTER ELEVEN

THE LATE-MORNING SUN blinded Tracey. She shielded her eyes with one hand and stood back, not certain what to say, or what to do. She figured if Manny needed anything, he'd let her know. Until then, she'd stay out of the way.

"Tell me again, precisely, the sequence of events, Bubba."

Worry lines creased Manny's forehead, and dark circles from fatigue hung under his eyes. That wasn't surprising. They'd only had about an hour and a half of sleep before Bubba called.

She and Manny had eaten breakfast in the truck, after driving through a fast-food place. He'd refilled the gas tank once, but beyond that, they'd been on the road for hours.

"We loaded the horse into the trailer, right after the paperwork was signed. Couldn't have been more than twenty minutes after you and Tracey left. When I stopped for gas on the way back to the Flying Horse, I checked on him. He looked nervous, but okay. When I got back here, I unloaded him right away and he ran in the pasture most of the rest of the day." Bubba hitched his pants.

"I put him in the stable around dusk," one of the hands contributed. "He was fine then."

"When was the last time anyone saw him?"

"I always check on my horses before I go to bed," Bubba said.

Mary came out from the house, expression drawn, features pale. Bubba paused for a few seconds, long enough to give her a worried look.

She moved to Bubba's side and he dropped his arm across his wife's shoulders and drew her close. Tracey felt a surge of pity for the woman, recalling she'd seen Bubba in much the same stance with Billie Jo Dumont at the Longhorn Coffee Shop just a few days earlier.

"What time would you say it was when I went out to the stables to check on the animals, sugar?"

Mary looked up at her husband. "Ten. Maybe ten-thirty."

"And you didn't notice anything out of the ordinary then?"

Bubba shook his head. "Not a thing."

"And you found him right before you called me?"

"Yep."

"And you just felt like taking a stroll out to the barn in the middle of the night? Do you do that often?"

"Any time I can't sleep. Any crime in that, son?" Bubba demanded, narrowing his eyes.

"No, sir," Manny replied easily. "Just trying to help you figure out what might have caused your horse's death."

Mary managed a tight smile. "We appreciate your driving all the way back from Corpus on such short notice, Manny," she said, and gave her husband a gentle pinch in the ribs. "We're grateful to you," Mary continued. "Isn't that right, Al?"

"Yeah. Right."

"Do you need me for anything else?" the ranch hand asked.

"No," Bubba said. "You go on ahead and do whatever it was you were doin'."

"Actually, I'd like you to stick around for a few minutes," Manny interjected, holding up a hand. "I may have a few more questions."

"Now listen here..." Bubba began. But at another pinch from Mary, he said nothing further.

Mary excused herself to make iced tea for everyone.

"I'd like to take another look at the horse," Manny said.

"Go on ahead," replied Bubba.

Tracey followed Manny and the other two men inside the stables. She didn't really want to be there, but felt compelled to stand by Manny, especially after everything they'd shared the night before.

Manny knelt in the straw, next to the unmoving horse. Tears welled in her eyes as she watched him run his hands along the animal's once-sleek flanks.

The stable seemed unnaturally silent. Somewhere outside, an airplane droned. She heard Manny's deep sigh. Scents of hay and sweat and horse manure hung in the air. But other, overshadowing odors assaulted her senses . . . those of fear and death.

She didn't know how Manny managed to deal with it. Tears clogged her throat at the sight of the horse lying on the straw, glazed eyes open wide, mouth hanging slack.

"He ate well," Bubba said. "Least that's what one of the boys said." Bubba hitched his pants again. Then he spit. "Damn. I just can't believe this. Here's my chance to dig my way out of this financial mess and then this happens. Damn."

"Is the ranch hand who fed the animals still here?"

"Naw. He went to see his ma for the rest of the weekend."

"Call him, tell him I want to talk to him."

"When?"

"Just as soon as I possibly can." Manny pushed to his feet. "I'll have to do a complete autopsy."

"Hell no!" Bubba said, adjusting his hat farther back on his head.

"I beg your pardon?" Manny dug a hand into his back pocket.

"I ain't got the money lyin' around to cover that kind of expense."

Bubba's attitude toward the death caused Tracey's opinion of him to drop by several more notches.

"I won't send you a bill," Manny said. "I want to get to the bottom of this."

"I don't know if that's necessary, son."

"Look, Bubba, a horse, apparently in perfect health, dropped dead in your stable early this morning. That may not be too much to worry about, except for the fact one of your llamas died just last week. Two and two are adding up to a whole lot more than four."

"What the hell you sayin', son?"

Manny said smoothly, "Maybe you got a bad batch of feed. Or maybe there's something going on we should know about." Manny looked the older man square in the eye. "And if you're going to be breeding championship quarter horses for racing, you want to know if there's something in this environment that's dangerous to them. Right?"

Bubba nodded, but said nothing.

"Besides, a vet's report will be required by the insurance company. Did you have time to take out a policy on the horse yet?"

Bubba's gaze slid away and he focused on a point somewhere over Manny's right shoulder. With thick fingers that were trembling from the heat and the shock, he wiped away a trickle of sweat that was slowly finding its way around the furrows in his forehead. "I've been so upset about the death, I hadn't even thought about the insurance. Hell, I hope they don't give me a hard time. It's bad enough to lose a prized animal like...well, you know how it is."

Manny *did* know the trauma of losing an expensive head of livestock, or a valued pet. And he could see that Bubba was truly upset about the horse's death. So he dispensed with further questions, and made arrangements about picking up the animal's body for transport to the autopsy. Then he took Tracey by the hand and headed for the truck.

Mary came out of the house, intercepting them along the way, a pitcher in one hand, a tray of glasses balanced in the other. "No tea?"

"No, thanks," Manny said. "We need to be on our way."

She smiled softly once again. "In that case, thank you for everything."

Manny didn't acknowledge the statement. Instead, he opened the door for Tracey.

"Are you okay?" she asked, when they were off the Gibsons' property.

"Yeah," he said distractedly. His tone and the look in his eye discouraged further conversation.

He pulled to a halt in front of Señora Sanchez's home and turned off the ignition. A few seconds later, he dropped his forehead to the top of the steering wheel.

"Manny?"

He didn't respond.

Tracey debated what to do. She couldn't decide whether to try and get him to talk, or to leave him to his own thoughts.

A few minutes later, he looked at her. "I'm sorry, Tracey. I'm not very good company."

"Care to come up for a while?" she asked quietly.

"No." He shook his head. "I've got to arrange to have the horse brought in for the autopsy."

As if to add emphasis to his words, he turned over the engine and it roared to life, the sound unnaturally loud in what had been a deafening silence.

Tracey hated to leave him like this. Her hand hesitated on the door handle. "Thanks for a wonderful weekend."

"Sure."

She opened the door, trying to ignore the feeling of rejection that crept over her.

"Hey, Trace?"

"Yeah?"

"Thanks for being there for me."

She climbed out of the cab, then closed the door. Manny drove off without a backward glance, and the pain of not being needed or wanted shot through her. Upstairs, in the privacy of her apartment, she gave in to tears for the second time in as many hours.

MINDLESSLY, Tracey rearranged the boots on the displays, adding a new design and taking away one that hadn't sold as well as she'd hoped. She had plenty of work to do, trying to collect on a check that had bounced, billings to mail, boots to ship out of state and the monthly inventory report. But when she tried to concentrate on work, her mind drifted.

Around noon, Serena arrived, her own lunch packed in a brown paper bag.

"I checked my answering machine and heard your good news," Serena said, letting the door close behind her. "A record-breaking week. Congratulations! You've brought your magic touch."

With the death of Bubba's horse and the fact Manny hadn't returned a call she'd made, Tracey'd almost forgotten her message to Serena about how well the boot store was doing. Tracey smiled, even though her heart wasn't in it.

"What's the matter?" Serena asked, brow furrowing into a frown. "You're not as up as you sounded on the machine. And you don't look so hot, either."

"Bubba Gibson's new horse died for no apparent reason early Sunday morning."

Serena looked confused.

"Manny seems to be taking it kind of personally."

"The quarter horse Bubba just bought in Austin so he could get in the racing business?"

"No." Tracey shook her head. "He bought another one Saturday morning in Corpus Christi."

"And it was dead within twenty-four hours?" Serena asked, shocked.

Tracey nodded, then adjusted one of the displays to a better angle.

"But that's not all, is it?"

Serena's perceptiveness didn't surprise Tracey.

"Manny?" When Tracey didn't answer, Serena added, "I think it's past time for a heart-to-heart. I brought my lunch. We can talk and eat at the same time."

Serena and Tracey headed for the back room. Both grabbed a can of soda to combat the not unusual fall heat wave. Then Tracey shook two aspirin from the bottle she'd purchased yesterday. The headache she'd woken up with was building to painful proportions.

"How did it go in Corpus Christi?" Serena asked, after they were settled at one of the worktables.

Tracey swallowed the tablets with a drink of her soda, then answered truthfully, "His parents were obviously as impressed with me as mine were with Manny." She rubbed her throbbing temples unconsciously.

"I hope you two aren't going to let that bother you," Serena said. "There are plenty of parents who don't approve of the people their children date."

"It's easy to be cavalier and pretend it doesn't matter," Tracey said. "And I would never stop seeing Manny because my parents have a hang-up about my dating someone who isn't the same race or religion."

"But?"

Tracey peeled a banana, not feeling hungry but knowing she had to eat something. "But I've always been close to my parents and it hurts to have them act this way."

Serena nodded in sympathy. "And what about his parents? You indicated they weren't a whole lot better."

"I think they were shocked that Manny didn't bring home a nice Hispanic girl for them to meet. In fact, Manny and his mother had words before we left. I don't think Señor Hernandez was as upset as his wife, but he wasn't all that thrilled either." Tracey sat with shoulders hunched forward in dejection.

"But none of this is the real issue, is it?"

"Damn, I wish you wouldn't do that to me."

Serena laughed. "You were just as unforgiving when I first started dating Cal, as I recall."

Tracey really did need someone to talk to. "Manny hasn't called since he dropped me back at my place yesterday morning. I called his home last night and got no answer, and I left a message at the clinic this morning."

"Just how close are you and Manny, anyway?"

She looked directly at Serena. "Closer than I've been with a man since college."

Serena's eyes opened wide. "Are you saying..." She trailed off.

"I'm saying I'm more than a little bit in love with him."

"God, Tracey," Serena said. "To my knowledge, you haven't even kissed a guy in four years."

"Until Manny." She tossed the banana peel in the garbage can. "I don't know, Serena. I'm confused. When he got the call about the horse, he shut me out completely. As if what we shared over the weekend didn't matter at all. And it mattered a great deal, at least to me."

"Give him a chance, Trace. He's probably worried sick trying to figure out what's going on with the horse, plus his parents and everything. I'm sure he'll call when he gets a chance."

Tracey looked at her friend, unconvinced.

"Look, why don't you take the rest of the day off? Go home, relax, kick that headache that's kicking you."

"No, I'll be fine."

"Go," Serena instructed. "I have work to do here, anyway."

Tracey didn't feel like arguing. Besides, she really hadn't accomplished much at the shop all morning, anyway. "Are you sure?"

"Go."

She dropped the uneaten banana in the trash, on top of the peel. After showing Serena the status of the work she'd been doing, Tracey picked up her purse and headed for the door. "Thanks, Serena."

Serena watched her friend climb behind the wheel of the car. Such a pessimistic attitude was unlike Tracey. And though she didn't like to interfere, Serena picked up the phone and dialed Cal's number. Manny's reputation as a lady-killer had never affected her opinion of him before, but this time, the woman involved was Serena's best friend.

"THANKS FOR COMING," Manny said, popping the top on a beer and handing it to his friend.

"Sounds serious," Cal said, taking the can from Manny.

Manny twisted the cap off a bottle of cola and poured it over the ice in a glass. Both men took a seat in Manny's kitchen, legs sprawled in front of them.

"So what's going on?"

"This thing with Bubba's animals is eating me up," Manny admitted.

"Yeah, I heard rumors down at the Longhorn yesterday evening. Then Serena came home from the boot store tonight after talking with Tracey."

Manny let some of the cold liquid slip down his throat. "Unfortunately, rumors about the death aren't just rumors."

"What happened?"

"That's the damnedest thing. I don't have a clue. You've been around horses your entire life," Manny said. "I was hoping you might have a perspective on this that I'm overlooking."

"You did an autopsy?"

"A real thorough one." In fact, he'd spent the entire day working on the case.

"Serena said Tracey told her Bubba protested that he couldn't afford one."

"I did it pro bono," Manny said. "I want to find out why a perfectly healthy horse—or at least a horse that appeared to be in perfectly good health— would drop dead in the middle of the night."

"Heart failure?" Cal surmised.

"No doubt about that," Manny agreed. "I came to that conclusion this afternoon."

"Go on," Cal urged, crossing his boots at the ankle. "You obviously think there's more here than meets the eye."

"Yep. Heart failure is the official cause of death. At least that's what's probably going on the certificate."

"But?"

"Heart failure is a catchall term for anything that goes wrong. I want to know why he had heart failure."

"Maybe he wasn't all that healthy to begin with," Cal said. "Maybe something could have been disguised by the seller long enough to screw up your initial examination."

Manny nodded. "It's a possibility. There're plenty of drugs out there. But I checked for those and there were no traces of anything. No, there's something else...."

Cal sat up a little straighter. "What do you think it could be?"

"Hell, I don't know." Manny finger combed his hair back from his forehead. It had been a hellishly long night, and an even longer day. "Between you and me, Cal, this whole damn thing feels more than a little coincidental."

"What do you mean?"

"Bubba lost a llama not long ago."

"So you're looking for a connection?"

"Maybe a virus, contaminated feed, something like that. If it's anything along those lines, I need to figure out what it is and put a stop to it before any more animals die at the Flying Horse."

"Are you suggesting someone might have poisoned those two animals?"

A drop of moisture ran down the side of the glass, pooling into Manny's palm. "I'm not suggesting anything." He took another drink. "But I'm sure as hell not ruling anything out, either."

"If you suspect someone poisoned those two animals, you're missing a motive," Cal reminded Manny.

"Motive and a whole lot more. If, and I stress if, it's poisoned feed, it could very well be accidental.

There's nothing to say it would be criminally motivated.''

Manny was thinking out loud. "And yet, if it's accidental, why don't I have an epidemic on my hands? It's been nearly a week since the llama died. All the ranchers around here buy from the same feed store. And Bubba just brought the new horse home yesterday, hardly enough time for a toxic amount of chemicals to build up."

Cal whistled. "Unless they were already there."

"Unless they were already there," Manny agreed. "I've sent samples of blood to Houston for a toxicology report to double-check. My lab isn't foolproof, so I could have missed something. But I think this case is too important to write off."

"I've seen horses drop dead for no apparent reason before," Cal said. "More than once on the rodeo circuit. Lynn even lost one of her horses not too long ago. Remember?"

"Yeah, I thought about that. He was under my care, too."

"Hey, don't blame yourself. Horses get old, tired, overworked. Everything dies sooner or later."

Manny tipped his head in acknowledgment.

"But you're suspicious about this one."

"Maybe I'm just taking it too seriously." Manny drained the glass, then put it on the drainboard. "Hell, Cal, if it wasn't for the llama, I'd have just performed a standard autopsy and called it an act of God.''

"But you can't this time?"

He shook his head. "I wish to hell I could."

The phone rang. Tracey? He hadn't talked to her all day and realized he missed the sound of her voice. Missed it like hell.

He grabbed it before the second ring... and was more than a little disappointed to hear Bubba on the other end, asking if the autopsy had revealed anything. "Nothing yet, but it'll take a while on the toxicology report. I'll get that certificate to you just as soon as I can."

Bubba muttered something, then said goodbye and hung up.

"Sorry I couldn't be of more help," Cal said, crushing the can in his hand. "Let me know what you come up with. In the meantime, I've got a date with a wonderful lady who won't speak to me for a week if I don't make it to dinner."

"Tell her I said hello."

"I will," Cal promised. At the door, he turned back to face Manny. "Not that it's any of my business or anything, but Serena sent Tracey home sick from the boot store this afternoon."

Manny's heart twisted. "Is she okay?" Even as Cal stood at the door, Manny reached for his keys on a hook near the back door.

"Serena said it didn't appear to be much to worry about. Just a virus or something. Catch you later."

Cal climbed into his truck. At least Serena would be pleased with him for mentioning Tracey went home early. Before he'd headed to Manny's, Serena had wangled that promise. Lord, but he had trouble denying her anything, especially once she set her mind to convincing him she was right.

But he would bet dollars to boots that Tracey would take an awl after him if she ever found out he'd interfered in her relationship with Manny.

"MANNY!" TRACEY SAID, obviously shocked.

She looked pale and very fragile in an oversize T-shirt that hung down to the middle of her thighs.

"You going to invite me in? Or are you too sick for company?"

"No...I mean, yes..." She held open the door. "Come in."

A novel lay open on the coffee table, spine up. A rerun of a sixties comedy blared on the television, and a box of tissues sat on the couch next to the blanket she'd obviously been cocooned in.

"I heard you weren't feeling well," he commented when she closed the front door behind them.

"Cal?" Tracey demanded.

"Cal came by."

"Did he tell you to come and see me?"

He noticed her eyes had narrowed. Obviously, she hadn't wanted news of her illness to get back to him. And that infuriated him. Working to keep his anger in check, he carefully responded, "No." He took a seat on the couch, next to her blanket. "All he said was that you went home sick this afternoon. I came by because I was concerned about you."

"Well, I'm fine." She sat next to him.

"You look tired."

"I'm always tired after work."

"But you went home early."

She shrugged.

"Look, Trace, does this have anything to do with us?"

"Us?" she echoed in exaggerated surprise. "There is no 'us,' Manny. At least not that I'm aware."

If it hadn't been for the fact that her eyes were bloodshot and dark smudges tinged the area beneath them, he might have bought the fact she was as unconcerned as she was trying to appear. "There sure as hell is an 'us,' Tracey."

"Really? Couldn't prove that by me."

He turned toward her, capturing her shoulders with the bite of his fingers. Her eyes flashed with an emotion he couldn't determine. Hell, the way things were going for him today, it was probably anger and nothing more. "If there isn't an us, then what was last weekend?"

"A weekend," she said. "Between two people who happened to be attracted to each other."

"That may be all it was to you, *querida,* but it was a hell of a lot more as far as I'm concerned."

"Oh. And what's that? Another notch in your bedpost?"

Anger, swift and sure, sliced through him. His grip tightened on her and his fingers were sinking deeper into her flesh. "You are not and will never be a notch in my bedpost."

"Then why haven't you called?" Her eyes continued to flash. "And why have you shut me out like I mean nothing to you?"

Hurt. Tracey was hurt. Because of him. He began to loosen his hold as realization dawned on him. She couldn't be hurt if she didn't care. Although her body was stiff and offered no encouragement, he took her in his arms and held her against his chest.

She resisted for a few seconds, then began to relax.

Manny stroked her hair and kneaded her shoulders where his fingers had dug. "I've been busy, *querida.* Nothing more. I performed the autopsy on Bubba's horse and delivered some tissue samples to the lab in Austin. And if you took that to mean I don't care, then I'm sorry."

He buried his face in the sweetness of her hair, so that his words were muffled as he continued. "I'm not accustomed to sharing my feelings, my concerns with anyone. I was raised to be tough, Tracey." He held her a little away from him, then stroked his thumb down the path of a tear.

"I've never had anyone in my life who matters to me as much as you do. I admit to not knowing where to start or even how to let you in. But I'm sure determined to commit myself to trying. I care about you, Tracey. And for you, I'm going to try to learn."

CHAPTER TWELVE

"SO SOON?" Bubba demanded.

"The sooner the better," the voice on the other end of the phone said.

Bubba ground out a four-letter word.

"That vet of yours is no fool. You're gonna have to move quick if you want him off your butt."

"Hell, I figured he'd go for the fact somethin' was wrong with the animal when we brought it back from Corpus."

"But he didn't. And now he's looking for a connection. Unless you don't need the money...in which case you could wait a couple of months, till it doesn't look so suspicious."

Bubba swore again. "I can't wait."

"I didn't figure you could."

"Look, my boys have the night off. They ain't gonna be around."

"You want me to come out around six?"

"Yeah."

"And I suggest you get rid of that vet before he digs too deep, you know what I'm saying? He's too nosy for my liking. And yours, too. It's your ass that's on the line, after all."

Bubba balled his fist at his side. If he didn't need the money so damn bad...

"You listening, Bubba?"

"I hear you." The rustle of clothing caught his attention. He pivoted, seeing his wife silhouetted in the doorway. "Gotta go." He hung up, then slid his thumbs under the belt loops in order to tug up his pants.

"Who was that?"

"No one for you to worry about, hon."

"Al..."

He held up his hands. "I swear, not a thing to worry about."

"Was that about the horse?"

Bubba winced. Lordy, lyin' was becoming a habit with him. But sometimes he didn't have a choice. "Yeah. I guess them toxicology reports didn't show nothin'. Manny came by this morning with the official death certificate."

Mary let a breath spill out her lips. "Good."

"Now we can get some money from the insurance to help buy a new horse. Yes, sirree, Mary, that dynasty is gonna save us."

"I sure hope you're right, Al."

"I am," he insisted. "Don't worry your pretty little self no more."

She offered a tentative, trusting smile. But he saw she didn't look convinced.

SWEETIE SKITTERED, dodging away from Manny, as if understanding that Manny and Tracey intended to take her away from her comfortable new home. Manny moved a little closer, talking softly to the animal while Tracey watched.

"That's it," he crooned. "Take it easy, Sweetie. We'll have this over soon enough."

Sweetie swung around and tried to take a chunk out of Manny's buttocks. He moved out of the way with not even a second to spare.

Tracey laughed.

"Think you can do better?"

"Let me try. I can't do a whole lot worse than you've been doing for the past fifteen minutes."

"Be my guest." He stood back, folding his arms across his chest, prepared to enjoy the show.

Tracey offered a handful of food as a bribe. The deer sniffed Tracey's hand, then stomped away. "Come on, Sweetie," she begged. "If you cooperate, you'll be back frolicking with all your deer friends by dark."

"Cute, Cotter," Manny said.

Tracey extended her hand again toward the animal. "I promise, Sweetie. You won't have to put up with this obnoxious vet and his mean ol' needles any longer."

The doe evidently wasn't convinced, and wanted nothing to do with leaving the barn. But after a few seconds, she returned to Tracey, lured by the food being offered.

While the deer munched, Tracey petted her, stroking the length of her neck. "Hand me the rope," she said to Manny. But the instant Manny reached over to hand it to Tracey, Sweetie bared her teeth. And this time managed to take a bite out of his sleeve.

"She's become a terror," Manny said, rubbing his arm and examining the ragged hole.

"According to rumor, you have this much trouble getting rid of most of the women in your life."

He moved around to the far side of Tracey, away from nipping teeth. Then he dropped a kiss on Tracey's forehead. "I think tales of my prowess have been greatly exaggerated. Besides, there's one woman in here I sure as hell don't want to get rid of."

Tracey rose on tiptoe to accept his second kiss. Sweetie took the opportunity to run the few steps back to the corner of the barn.

"I think this is a job for super rodeo champ," Manny said.

"Cal," both said simultaneously.

"He was home when I talked to Serena earlier," Tracey said. "Want me to give him a call?"

"And leave me here alone with a demented deer? No way."

Tracey couldn't help but laugh.

When Manny went to use the phone, Sweetie mellowed. She nuzzled Tracey, rubbing her head against Tracey's leg as if asking to be petted once again.

"You're spoiled," Tracey told her, as she continued to stroke the animal's graceful neck. "I'm going to miss you, but you'll be better off in the wild."

"Cal's on his way," Manny announced, as he reentered the barn. "You ungrateful creature," he admonished the deer, but his tone was gentle and affectionate, revealing that he, too, would miss Sweetie.

The deer showed her teeth again, but the expression appeared more like a smile than an act of aggression or ingratitude.

Within a few minutes, Serena arrived with Cal, who had a lasso in hand.

"So where's Killer?" Cal asked.

"Killer?" Tracey echoed in mock horror. "Her name's Sweetie and it suits her."

"Tell my ripped shirt," Manny said.

"It's only a little hole," Tracey assured him, but couldn't resist teasing. "The ragged look is in style this fall."

Cal chuckled, but it was Sweetie who got the last laugh. It took all four adults almost a half hour to catch her and load her into the trailer. Cal's jeans were the only casualty.

"Thanks for coming out," Manny said. "I could have tranquilized her, but I hated the thought of doing that. I wouldn't have wanted to let her go until she'd completely recovered from the drug."

"Happy to help," Cal replied, casting a wry glance at his pants. "Sure you can manage from here?"

"I've just got to decide where to let her out."

"I'm sure you can find some of her relatives at the Hole in the Wall," Serena suggested. "She'll be able to find herself a male friend to keep her from missing you too much. I've heard about that potent Latin charm."

Tracey and Serena exchanged conspiratorial winks.

"It's not me she'll be missing, but this nice dry barn and all that grain Tracey's been stuffing her with," Manny commented. "Foraging on leaves and berries is going to be quite a comedown."

When the sound of Cal's pickup faded in the distance, Manny asked, "Ready?"

"Sure."

They drove to the Hole in the Wall and ran into Scott as he emerged from the main entrance. When they asked for his permission to let Sweetie loose on the ranch grounds, he went them one better.

"I've got an idea where you can unload her," he informed them as he peered into the trailer. "I saw some fresh deer tracks early this morning down by the creek. Come on, and I'll show you."

Manny drove the truck and trailer to the spot Scott indicated, and opened the trailer door.

Sensing there were other deer in the area, Sweetie coolly strolled out of the trailer, hopped to the ground and looked around with interest.

"The picture of tranquillity," Tracey said.

"Tell that to my shirt."

Tracey ran her palm around the animal's long, narrow nose for the last time. "Goodbye, Sweetie."

The deer licked Tracey's cheek with its thin, black tongue, then turned and walked toward the woods. But before disappearing into the trees, she stopped and looked back at Manny, her huge brown eyes unblinking and that curious animal grin on her face. With a last flick of her stubby tail, she disappeared into the scrub oak thicket.

"I'm going to miss having her around," Manny said.

"I don't think you're lacking in the female companionship area," Scott teased.

"You're right," Manny agreed, placing his hands on Tracey's shoulders and gently massaging. She relaxed with a sigh.

"Well, ma'am, it looks like it's just you and me at the house from now on."

He turned her in his arms. She looked up at him, and read the promise of the future in his expression. Though neither had spoken words of love, Tracey didn't doubt they would soon.

"I TALKED to my mother this morning," Tracey said, taking a deep drink from her glass of the Longhorn's special iced tea. She wrinkled her nose at the flavor, then stirred in another packet of sugar. "She's starting to accept the fact I'm seeing you." But just because she was becoming more accepting of the relationship didn't mean she liked it, Tracey added silently. But she chose not to voice that bit of information.

"I'm glad to hear that," Manny said sincerely.

"I think she's having trouble with the idea I don't listen to her like I used to. That and the fact I wouldn't marry the preacher's son as she'd hoped I would."

"The preacher's son?"

Tracey squeezed the juice from the slice of lemon into her tea. "Fine Southern Baptist gentleman."

"Good Lord! No wonder she had problems with a Catholic."

"Well, at least she's dropped the wedding plans. That's a start." Tracey grinned.

"My father was impressed with your Spanish," Manny said. "I didn't know you were fluent."

"I guess it never came up before."

Further conversation was interrupted by Nora's arrival, green order pad in hand and pen tucked behind her ear. "Y'all ready?"

They gave Nora their order, but before she took off, Manny asked, "How's Mary doing? I talked to Bubba like you asked. Didn't seem to do a heck of a lot of good."

Nora reached behind her for the pitcher of tea on the counter, then refilled Tracey's glass. After glancing around to make sure everyone was engrossed in their own conversations, Nora leaned closer.

"I appreciate your trying, Manny. Mary's keeping up a brave front, but I know she's distressed. She said something about Cody Hendricks at the bank setting them up with a small loan to help tide them over." Nora shook her head. "She talked to Bubba about selling some of his land, but he won't consider it. I don't know, Manny. I wish someone could talk some sense into that man. Before it's too late.''

Nora moved away, but quickly returned a few minutes later with their salads. While they ate, Manny filled Tracey in on the developments of the case involving Bubba's horse. He mentioned the clean toxicology report.

''It doesn't make sense. Medically, there's no reason that horse shouldn't be walking around, or even training to run a race.''

Tracey was on her last bite of salad when a man she didn't recognize hurried over to their table.

''Manny! I've been looking all over for you, *amigo.*''

''Eddie, *qué pasa?*'' Manny introduced her to Eddie, a hand at the Flying Horse Ranch.

''We tried to reach you on the beeper, man, but you never called us back.''

Manny unclipped the beeper, then checked the display. ''Damn. The batteries must be dead. What's the matter?''

''Another horse just died.''

Manny's fork clattered onto the table. ''*¡Madre de Dios!* When did this happen?''

''Jus' an hour or so ago, man. Señor Gibson, he's not takin' it too well . . . after the first horse 'n all.''

Manny swore softly and succinctly, using a Spanish word that was rapidly becoming familiar to Tracey.

"Tell Bubba I'm right behind you."

Eddie left and Manny turned to face her.

"Don't apologize," Tracey said. "Duty calls. I understand."

He wadded his napkin and tossed it in the nearly empty bowl of lettuce.

Tracey's heart sank. From the way Manny's eyes had narrowed when Eddie talked, she realized they were both thinking along the same lines.

"Nora!"

"Yeah, Manny?"

"Cancel our dinners."

"You got trouble?"

"'Fraid so."

"No problem." She nodded.

He dropped enough money on the table to cover the bill and a big tip. "I hope you weren't starving," he said to Tracey.

"We'll eat later."

"Want me to run you back to the shop before I head out to the Flying Horse?"

"No. I know you're in a hurry. And I'd like to go with you." She was rewarded by a grateful smile.

They rode in tense silence. Manny's knuckles were white where they gripped the steering wheel. He squealed to a stop in front of the barn.

Mary met them outside, her fingers twisted together. "It's Flying Wind," she said without preamble. "I found her dead not more than forty-five minutes ago."

Manny cursed again.

"Al's in the stables, questioning the hands."

Acid burned in Tracey's stomach as she and Manny followed Mary toward the long, low barn. This was becoming an all-too-familiar routine.

Bubba stopped in midsentence, hitched his pants, then said curtly, "Another one of my animals is dead, Manny." He slammed his fist into his opposite palm. "And I want to know what in the name of hell you're gonna do about it."

The hostility radiating from Bubba caused Tracey to take a step back.

"My animals ain't supposed to drop dead, Manny. They're supposed to be healthy. *You* checked them. Now they're dead!"

"At this point, I don't have any answers," Manny said. "Not until I perform an autopsy on this horse and have the lab run some tests."

"More tests?" Bubba sneered. "Just what I need. Fancy tests when my animals are dyin'. Your fancy tests didn't help none last time, did they?"

"Al!" Mary scolded.

"Well, I'm tired of our future dyin' on us, sugar. Every time Manny stops by, something bad happens. And I ain't gonna stand for it no more."

"Are you trying to say something, Bubba?" Manny asked with a menacing quietness.

"This makes three of my animals that died while under your care. Flying Wind here was my ticket to fame and fortune." Bubba moved a wad of chew with his tongue. "You said she was a sound investment. I believed you, trusted your word when I shouldn't have."

"I said she appeared to be healthy," Manny corrected. "Without a thorough exam, it would have been impossible... and irresponsible... for me to have made a firm prognosis."

"Yeah, well, that little mistake of yours cost me all my working capital... and then some."

"If you recall, I advised you might find a better deal if you continued to shop."

"If any more of my animals just up and die like that, I won't have any ranch left to worry about. I'm bringing in a veterinarian from Austin to look at the cattle, and make sure there wasn't anything else you missed on your routine visits that will cost me a fortune. You see, Manny, I ain't *tryin'* to tell you nothin'. I *am* tellin' you that we won't be requirin' your services no more. And I'll be spreading the word to my friends, too.''

Tracey gasped, and instinctively searched Manny's face. A tic of annoyance beat in his temple.

"I don't want you touching Flying Wind," Bubba went on.

"That's your prerogative, of course, but—"

"Damn straight."

Manny continued, "I'd like the courtesy of finishing this case, however. If you want me to work with your new vet, I'd be glad to."

"I don't know about—"

"I think that's fine, Manny," Mary interrupted. "You're right, you do deserve that courtesy."

Bubba tipped back his hat and scowled, but he didn't contradict his wife. Again, a feeling of distaste for Bubba rose in Tracey. Manny was a damn fine vet. Everyone said so.

"I'll arrange transportation of Flying Wind within the hour," Manny said.

"You do that," Bubba said. "And don't you be holding up any of my paperwork."

"Wouldn't dream of it," Manny responded.

Tracey wondered how he could manage to be so cool and calm.

"Tracey?" Manny called, turning away from the Gibsons. "Let's go."

Tracey joined him at the door.

"Oh, by the way," Manny said, stopping and turning back around. "Mary said you've questioned the ranch hands."

"I did."

"And is there any information you feel might be useful?"

He hitched his pants. "Not a thing. Same situation as when my other horse died." Bubba expelled the chew in a runny, brown lump.

Manny nodded, then escorted Tracey back to the truck. He drove in silence, his forehead burrowed into worried lines.

Tracey told him he could drop her back at the shop.

"Okay. I want to get right to work on this."

When Manny stopped in front of the shop, she reached for the door, but he placed a restraining hand around her lower wrist. "I'm not shutting you out, Trace. I promise."

She nodded, trying to reconcile her need to be needed with his need to be alone. When he pulled her closer, she willingly gave herself over to the pleasure of his kiss.

This time, however, she sensed an overriding urgency in his touch. Responding in kind, she wrapped her arms around him, mindless of the gear knob digging into her ribs. Or the fact that anyone could be watching.

Manny thrust his tongue into her mouth and she groaned from deep inside. The passionate kiss was a need of Manny's she could meet.

All too soon, he released her. Her breathing was erratic, but his was, too.

"I'll call you tomorrow," he promised, dragging a lock of hair back from his forehead.

"If I can do anything..." She left the promise open.

"Thanks."

This time, when she opened the door, he let her go.

"BUBBA FIRED MANNY?" Nora asked in shock. "Now wait a minute. Let me turn off the sign. I don't think we want any interruptions."

Nora pulled the chain to turn off the neon Open sign, then flipped over the more standard cardboard sign. After that, she poured two cups of coffee and returned to the booth where Mary sat, her hand shaking.

"It was awful," Mary said, pulling out a piece of tissue from where she'd tucked it in her sleeve. "I've never been so humiliated in my life, and *that's* saying something!"

Nora took a sip of coffee and waited for Mary to continue.

"This has been one of the worst months ever," Mary said, tracing the cup handle with her finger. "Al wanted to make a fresh start." She looked at Nora with complete openness. "He took every penny we had, Nora, and a few we didn't have to buy those two quarter horses. And now they're dead. We're in debt so far it'd take nothing short of a miracle to save us."

Nora shook her head.

"Then his firing Manny was the final straw."

"What do you mean, final straw?"

"I've decided to go away for a bit, Nora."

Nora's jaw hung slack. "You're gonna leave?"

Mary squared her shoulders. "I am. I have a good friend in Austin I can stay with. Until Allan Gibson realizes what his stubbornness has cost us, I don't want to see him again."

"Now," Nora said, "don't be doing anything rash, Mary. These things work themselves out."

"Did they for you?"

Nora had to admit Mary was right. "No. But I'll be in your corner, no matter what...." Nora let her thoughts trail off. She was the last person who would encourage a woman to stay in a situation where she was unhappy.

"That means a lot," Mary said.

"I wish you luck," Nora said sincerely.

The two talked for a few more minutes, then Mary said, "You've got to promise me you won't breathe a word of where I'm going to Al."

"My lips are sealed."

"I knew I could count on you."

Mary let herself out and Nora sank against the vinyl-backed seat. She was worried for Mary, and after what she'd just heard, Nora was concerned about Manny, too. Of one thing, she was certain. Bubba could be counted on to spread the news that he'd fired Crystal Creek's only veterinarian.

BUBBA WATCHED in shock as Mary lugged her suitcase up the stairs. Taking the steps two at a time, he followed her.

"Now just where in the hell do you think you're goin'?"

She opened a drawer, grabbed a handful of sturdy cotton lingerie and tossed it into the open piece of luggage.

"I asked where you think you're goin'," Bubba repeated. He folded his arms across his chest to prevent himself from grabbing his wife and shaking some sense into her as he wanted to.

Hell, he hadn't seen her this upset since sometime in the late sixties, when he'd lost her favorite cow in a poker game.

"I'm not telling you where I'm going," she said with uncharacteristic defiance.

"When are you coming back?"

"When I'm damn well ready. Maybe never."

Bubba's eyes opened wide. His wife didn't swear. Ever.

"I've tried to be supportive of you, Allan Gibson. I've even looked the other way, hoping you'd grow up, dump that silly Billie Jo and settle down, but you never did. Today was the last straw. Manny Hernandez is a good man and you know it." She grabbed a tissue from a box on the nightstand and wiped the tears from her face.

Seeing his wife like this nearly killed him. His anger evaporated. Suddenly, he just wanted to hold her, wanted to promise that everything would be all right and that the future could be like the past. He reached for her, but she shrugged him off.

"Don't!"

Bubba stepped back.

"Don't touch me!"

Helplessly, he allowed his arms to fall to his sides. She brushed by him, opened the closet door and pulled garments off hangers. Then she shoved them in the suitcase.

"I don't know what you think you've been do-ing or who you've been plotting with," she informed him, dumping a few more things in the case. "But I've got eyes, Al, and ears. And if you don't think I've noticed you've been up to something, you're wrong. Dead wrong."

Shock made his head reel. That his sweet, calm, predictable Mary was behaving like this was nearly incomprehensible.

"Don't worry. I don't know *exactly* what you've been up to, but I know enough to know I don't like it." She pointed a finger at him. "Not one bit." With a vicious yank, she finished zipping the luggage, then dragged it off the bed.

"Now, hon, let's just talk about this. There's no sense gettin' your pretty little self in a twist over nothin'. I'm jus' doin' my best to take care of you the way I've always done." His voice took on a note of desperation. "Jus' come downstairs with me. Hell, even better, I'll take you out to a restaurant for dinner. Give me another chance. What do you say, sugar?" He looked at her as earnestly as he knew how.

"I say goodbye, Allan Gibson."

She grabbed the piece of luggage by the strap and started pulling it away.

"Now, wait. You jus' can't up and leave."

"Watch me." At the top of the stairs, she picked up the case and carried it.

Bubba followed, not knowing what to say or do. As the front door slammed behind her, he'd never felt more helpless in his whole life.

You're a damn fool, his conscience mocked.

Pulling back the drape, he watched her climb into the car. It kicked up a cloud of dust as she floored the gas pedal, obviously anxious to get away from him.

Bubba sank a fist into the wall next to the window. He'd done it all for Mary's sake, he told himself. Every last bit of it. And for what?

The truth was, he was in so deep, there was no possible way to crawl out of the quagmire.

CHAPTER THIRTEEN

"ARE YOU the veterinarian?"

Manny looked up from his place behind the counter, where he was doing the billing. "Yes, I am."

The man, tall and thin like a stalk of cactus, and just as prickly, looked at his clipboard, then back at Manny. He squinted through a pair of wire-framed glasses.

"And you are?"

"Marvin Merritt." The man extended his hand and Manny shook it. "I'm an insurance adjuster from Austin."

"And you're here on behalf of—"

"Allan Gibson. I have a few questions for you, Mr. Hernandez, if you can spare the time."

"Come on back into my office."

Manny left the door open, since there were no customers. He sat behind his desk and rolled a pen between his fingers as he waited for the other man to get settled.

"You're the vet for the Flying Horse Ranch. Correct, Mr. Hernandez?"

"No. I *was* the vet. As I understand it, another veterinarian has been retained to service the ranch."

"I see." He scrawled a note. "What is the official cause of death of Mr. Gibson's two horses and a . . ." He checked his clipboard. "I believe it was a llama?"

"You've got my reports right there," Manny replied. "I assume you've read them."

"Yes," Merritt agreed easily enough. "I read 'em, but they don't say much."

"There's not much to say. Cause of death is listed as heart failure."

Merritt mopped his brow with a kerchief that stuck out of his suit coat pocket.

"Oh, come on, Mr. Hernandez. You and I both know that can mean anything, don't we?"

"I've included copies of the autopsy reports," Manny said. "They say the same thing."

"They weren't very specific." He squinted again, making his beady eyes appear even smaller. "Perhaps something was overlooked?"

"Are you insinuating something?" Manny leaned back in his seat. He was getting more than a little sick of the accusations he'd been hearing around town over the past few days.

As he'd expected, Bubba's big mouth had been running, and it was almost as though a line had been drawn down the middle of Main Street between those who believed Manny might have been negligent and those who believed the deaths were coincidental and nothing more.

Manny had worked hard for years to build a reputation, and he resented like hell the implications he'd been less than diligent.

"I'm not insinuating a thing," Merritt assured him, his long, thin fingers gripping the wooden clipboard. "It's just that I like to have all bases covered, if you know what I mean. As a veterinarian with a sterling reputation, you feel the same way, I'm sure. Right, Mr. Hernandez?"

Manny drummed his fingers on his desk as his blood pressure rose. Despite the man's smooth denial, he was obviously implying there was more to the case than appeared in Manny's reports.

"As best as I could determine through autopsies and toxicology reports run by a reputable firm in Austin, the deaths were strictly accidental."

"What do you know of Mr. Gibson's financial situation?"

"That it's none of my business and none of yours either." Manny didn't like Merritt. He liked his line of questioning even less. "Look, Mr. Merritt, if you have something to say, say it. Otherwise, all the information you need is in the papers you already have.''

''It's nothing like that,'' he assured Manny.

''Then if you'll excuse me, I have other commitments.'' He didn't actually have any appointments. In fact, since Bubba had made his nasty accusations at the Longhorn Coffee Shop several days before, business had dropped off drastically. But he'd be damned if he'd spend his time being interrogated by a toad.

''Surely.'' Merritt stood to leave. When he'd nearly reached the door, he stopped. ''Oh, there's another small matter.''

Manny expelled his breath in a deep, annoyed exhalation.

''Mr. Gibson says you personally checked out both horses before he invested the money in them.''

''That's correct.''

''And what did you find?''

''Nothing out of the ordinary.''

''Which means?''

''Exactly that. The horses appeared to be in fine shape.''

''So, in your professional opinion, you found no reason Mr. Gibson's horses or the llama should have suddenly died.''

Manny narrowed his eyes. He didn't know what Merritt was getting at, but he suspected the man was sharper than Manny had first given him credit for. In fact, he was echoing some of the same things that had passed through Manny's mind. "In my professional opinion, no, there was no reason that I could see for any of the animals to die so suddenly."

"And just one more thing."

There was that annoying squint again. Impatiently, Manny waited for Merritt to continue.

"Were either of the horses worth fifty thousand dollars?"

Fifty thousand! The figure stunned Manny, though he tried not to show it. He knew Bubba had paid a lot for both the horses, but he'd imagined nothing close to that figure. A strange feeling he couldn't name began to nag him. He recalled the conversation at the Longhorn Coffee Shop with Nora, about how Mary Gibson had been worried about their financial situation. And the way they'd taken a small loan recently.

"I'm not an expert on the value of racehorses."

"Thank you, Mr. Hernandez. You've been most helpful," Merritt said, evidently taking Manny's nonanswer as all the response he needed. He made a couple of notations on his yellow legal pad. "I'll be in touch if there's anything else I need from you."

Manny saw the man out, then returned to his office. He propped his booted feet on his desk, then, with a deep sigh of exhaustion, dragged a hand through hair that needed combing. Hell, he needed a shave too. When was the last time he'd thought about something so mundane as showering or sleeping?

Or eating?

He'd been neglecting his other cases—those that he still had. Manny picked up the file folder marked "Flying Horse" and started to thumb through the pages again. Maybe on the last five reads he'd missed something significant.

An hour or so later, he slammed it back down and came to his feet. Flying Wind's death was as much a mystery as those of the llama and the other horse . . . and Manny didn't like puzzles.

Things like this just didn't happen. Deaths always had logical explanations. Unfortunately, at the moment, he had none.

Whom could he talk to? Where could he go? He swiveled around in his chair and his gaze rested on his diploma. Texas A&M, the finest agricultural and animal husbandry university in the nation. Maybe he could find some answers there.

Deciding to head over to College Station the next day, he locked all his files away, then checked to make certain everything else was secure.

Manny looked at the clock and couldn't believe how late it was. He grabbed the fistful of messages lying on his desk and noticed that the top one had Tracey's name scrawled across it. It was dated yesterday. "Call me," he read.

Thoughts of Tracey paraded through his mind. Hell, he was probably in a lot of trouble there, too. He'd sworn not to shut her out, but he'd done it again and it wasn't intentional.

Clear as day, he remembered her saying, "If you need me, I'll be there for you...."

Manny squeezed his eyes shut. Yep. He definitely needed her. He locked up and headed outside.

The truck's cab was still warm from the day's heat. A plaintive country tune only rattled his nerves more, so he ejected the tape and chose one of Linda Ronstadt singing Spanish ballads. He drove automatically for ten minutes, before realizing his destination was Tracey's apartment.

He parked out front, glad to note her lights were on. Pocketing the keys, he headed upstairs. "It's Manny," he called, after knocking on the door.

She opened it almost instantly.

A soft robe hugged her body, the velour material ending just above her knees, leaving her tanned legs tantalizingly bare.

"Manny," she said. "I didn't expect you."

Damp strands of hair clung to her face and nape. An oddly haunting mixture of soap, shampoo and cologne teased his long-starved senses. "I'm sorry I haven't called."

Silently, she rubbed her hair with the ends of a towel.

"It's been a hellish couple of days."

She smiled, and he felt the first real relief since the whole ordeal had begun. "Come in."

She stepped back and his arm accidently grazed the softness of her breasts. A surge of passion choked him.

"Can I get you something to drink? I think there's a Corona left."

"No thanks."

"Did you eat dinner?"

"Today?"

"Today," she repeated.

"No."

"Yesterday?"

"I don't think so." He dragged his fingers through his hair. "I honestly don't remember."

"You must be starving," she said.

"Not really."

"You don't have to look so scared. I wasn't going to offer to cook. I can warm up some Chinese takeout leftovers."

He became conscious of his growling stomach.

"Sweet and sour shrimp," she said. "And an egg roll."

"Sold." Manny followed her into the kitchen and slouched onto a chair, folding his arms across his chest while she reheated the food. Within minutes, it was steaming.

"So, how's it going at the boot shop?" he asked, remorseful that his own problems had pushed all thoughts of her work out of his mind.

"Yesterday, Beverly picked up the boots she ordered for Jeff. You should see them. They turned out great."

She piled the food high on two plates, then handed him a set of chopsticks. "What do you want me to do with these?" he asked, holding them awkwardly.

"Eat."

"You've got to be kidding. I thought you were trying to feed me, not tease me."

She grinned mischievously, then took a knife and fork from the drawer. "There's a real art to eating with chopsticks. I'll teach you sometime."

"No thanks. I'll stick to what I know. I like to eat my food, not fight with it."

They carried their plates into the living room. Across from Manny, Tracey seated herself comfortably, curling her legs underneath her. The position exposed a bit more than a hint of thigh, and shortly, Manny discovered it was becoming difficult to swallow.

As usual, Tracey was disturbing his equilibrium. And he needed her more than he'd ever needed anyone in his life. "Trace," he said hoarsely.

With a knowing look, she crossed the room. He picked her up, draping her legs across his arms. Her hands locked behind his neck. Then he carried her to bed.

IN THE MIDDLE of the night, Manny stroked through the blunted ends of Tracey's hair. She murmured something, then snuggled deeper into his arms, her hands resting possessively on his body.

Sometime during the night, the realization had hit him, and hard.

He loved Tracey Cotter. And he wanted her to share her life with him. The hellish thing about it was, he dared not say anything about it until the situation with Bubba's livestock was cleared up. A town the size of Crystal Creek gossiped. The rumors flying about him and his abilities as a vet disturbed him, and he didn't want Tracey to get dragged down with him.

He had little doubt she'd stand by him. But it was his problem, and he knew it. Actually, this new situation dwarfed the other impediments to their relationship. Compared with the war he faced to clear his reputation, a few compromises about heritage and religion seemed insignificant.

"Manny?"

"Hmm?"

She moved away, blinking her eyes a little sleepily. "Want to talk about it?"

Tracey always managed to cut right through his defenses. Nestled warmly against him, she waited—waited for him to trust her enough to confide in her.

"Until this incident, my integrity has never been questioned." He caught one of her hands. "You know what gets me, Trace?"

She shook her head.

"I don't have the answers Bubba wants. Even *I'm* beginning to wonder if I might have done something wrong, if I overlooked a small detail. Anything."

"It would have shown up on the autopsies. In fact, didn't you say you compared the toxicology reports and found no traces of poison?"

"Nothing about this entire case is logical," Manny said. He dragged the errant lock of hair back from his forehead.

"Do you suspect foul play?"

Manny shrugged. "I don't know, Tracey. I just don't know. There's no evidence of anything out of the ordinary...."

"But..." she whispered into the night, her breath stirring against his chest.

"Bubba's horses were insured for a hell of a lot more than they were worth. More than double what he paid for them. And Nora mentioned the Gibsons' financial situation. Bubba needed that money badly." The insurance money could definitely have provided a motivation, he thought, but he was still no closer to the method that might have been used.

"Trust your instincts, Manny. If something feels wrong, it probably is."

"In this case, Trace, it's difficult to do that. There's no conclusive proof about anything."

"No matter what, I swear I'm on your side and that I'll stick by you."

He kissed her forehead. No doubt about it. It was love.

"Roll over," she instructed.

He did, hating to lose the feel of her in his arms. With slow circular motions, her small, but strong hands began to work some of the tension from his shoulders.

"*Querida,* I'm giving you three hours to stop that."

She laughed softly.

Thanks to Tracey, for a few hours during the long night, he slept.

MANNY HAD DISAPPEARED from the bed way before dawn stained the Texas sky. He'd told her he was driving to Texas A&M to spend however long it took in the library to find some answers. Unable to sleep once he left, Tracey showered, then drove to the Longhorn for breakfast.

"Mornin'," Nora greeted her warmly. "Coffee?"

"Just bring the pot and a straw," Tracey mumbled.

"That bad, huh?" she asked sympathetically, filling a cup to the rim.

Tracey picked up the cup and took a long drink, letting the steam bathe her face. "Perfect," she said with a sigh. Her first two swallows drained almost half the cup.

Nora refilled it, then said, "So, anything to eat this morning or just a jolt of caffeine?"

"A bowl of fruit?"

"Coming up."

In minutes, Nora returned with a mixture of fresh strawberries, peaches and melons. Tracey smiled her thanks, then went to the front counter to pick up a local newspaper.

She turned first to the comics, then checked her horoscope. Seeing nothing dire was predicted for the day, she flipped to the front page, noting a picture of Manny there, along with an article.

She scanned the headline, immediately losing her appetite. Local Vet Unable to Account for Mysterious Deaths. She let her fork drop against the side of the bowl, then pushed her breakfast aside.

The article was several paragraphs long. It recounted the deaths of the livestock at the Flying Horse Ranch, and mentioned the fact that Bubba Gibson had contracted with a vet in Austin to provide care for the rest of his animals. Somewhere near the end, the article also listed the names of other ranches that had followed suit.

Thankfully, Tracey noticed that the Hole in the Wall, the Double C and the Circle T weren't listed anywhere in the article. Losing those ranches could mean disaster for Manny's practice.

Another thought chased through her mind. Just because those ranches weren't mentioned, didn't mean they were definitely planning to retain Manny's services.

Tracey folded the page over angrily. She finished her coffee, but couldn't even summon a smile when Nora returned.

"What's the matter, honey?"

"Evidently you haven't seen the paper." Tracey once again opened to the offensive page and pointed to the article. She watched the expression on Nora's face change from one of disbelief, to shock, then finally to outrage.

"Well, I never," Nora said. "Has Manny seen this?"

"I doubt it. He left early this morning to drive to A&M."

"Don't let it bother you, honey," Nora said. "As soon as the next piece of gossip comes along, this will be forgotten."

"I know you hear people talk about everything here. How bad is it for Manny?" Tracey asked. "Be honest."

"Well, it's not easy to say. Lots of folks don't respect Bubba's opinion, and they don't care for the fact he so blatantly runs around on his wife." Nora tutted. "And news of his financial situation is pretty well-known, too. Some people think he's gotten vindictive since Mary left."

"Mary left?" Tracey echoed in disbelief.

"See? Not everything that happens in town spreads like a wildfire in July."

"But most of it isn't in the newspaper."

"I have to concede your point there."

"So where did Mary go?"

"She needed to get away for a while."

From Nora's tone and careful wording, Tracey suspected Nora knew exactly where Mary was, but had promised to keep the secret.

In the kitchen, a bell dinged. "Excuse me a minute." After delivering steak and eggs to a table, Nora returned to Tracey.

"Manny's well-liked and respected in this town," Nora said. "It'll pass. I promise."

"Thanks." After paying her bill, Tracey drove to work, surprised to find Serena already there.

"I gather you saw the paper?" Serena asked, without even so much as a good-morning.

Tracey felt her shoulders sag, though she tried not to let them. "Yeah, I saw it."

They went into the back room, where Serena had already brewed a pot of coffee. She poured them each a cup, then joined Serena at their table.

"Cal and J.T. figured you'd probably read the paper. I wanted to come by and offer moral support. I know this can't be easy."

"It's not," Tracey admitted, sipping excessively strong coffee. She wasn't complaining, though. She needed help this morning, and she'd take it from anywhere she could get it.

"How's Manny holding up?"

"As well as can be expected, considering he feels his career may be over. Evidently, his calls have dropped significantly in the past few days."

"Damn." Serena pushed back her hair from her face.

"He's worried, Serena," Tracey said, blowing the steam away from her face. "If he's slept eight hours in the past three days, I'd be surprised. But that's not the worst of it," Tracey continued. "Manny feels maybe some of the ranchers wouldn't have dropped him if he hadn't been Mexican-American."

Serena shook her head. "Gossip's the lifeblood in a town like this. If Manny had been born north of the Mason-Dixon Line, he would have been suspect because he was a damn Yankee."

Tracey nodded. Her friend had helped put things in perspective. "You know, I just wish I knew what to say to him. He's trying his best not to shut me out, but it's hard for him."

"Just be there," Serena urged. "What's important is that you stand behind him. He needs you now more than ever, Trace."

"I know."

"Listen, Cal's going to try and get over to see Manny today and talk to him about the situation."

"Meaning?"

"Cal and J.T. both want to let Manny know they're not intending to switch vets."

Tracey released a breath she hadn't realized was caught in her chest. "He probably won't be able to catch up with Manny until late this evening or tomorrow. He drove to A&M to do some research this morning. But I'm glad to hear the Double C won't be switching vets."

"I hope it helps, after he sees or hears about that article."

"I'm a little surprised J.T. opted to support Manny," Tracey commented. "Especially since he and Bubba have been friends for so many years."

Serena sighed. "Actually, there was a big family discussion about it last night. Hank was his crotchety self and really bent J.T.'s ear. I think you're right that J.T. has loyalties to his friend, but when faced with his grandfather, his son and his wife, he had to look at the facts, and the facts show accidental deaths happen. Manny's got an excellent record, and in the end that's what mattered.''

Tracey managed a wan smile. Serena always commented on how optimistic Tracey was, but right now, optimism was in short supply.

"It'll work out," Serena assured her.

Within a half hour, Serena was gone, and Tracey was forced to focus her energies on running the boutique, even though her heart truly wasn't in it. All morning, her thoughts kept returning to Manny. She hoped, more than anything, that he'd be able to come up with something—anything to clear his name.

THAT DAMN MARVIN MERRITT had been poking his nose around the Flying Horse, asking a lot of questions for the second day in a row, and Bubba was getting very tired of it.

Merritt strode from the barn, his clipboard tucked under his arm. "I have a final question before I turn the paperwork in."

Bubba moved the chew from one cheek to the other.

"I see from the photocopies you gave me that you paid far less than half the price of the value listed when you recently amended your coverage."

"I got me a bargain. Any crime in that?"

His faded blue eyes squinted. "Not as far as I'm concerned. I will, however, need to turn your file over to my supervisor." Merritt adjusted the bolo tie around his neck, then ran his finger under the starched collar of his shirt. "If we have any more questions, we'll be in touch. We should have a check cut and mailed out to you within thirty days."

"Thirty days?" Bubba exclaimed, aghast. "But I need mah money now, not in thirty days. I can't run a ranch without capital."

"These things take time, Mr. Gibson, I'm sure you understand."

"I've been payin' y'all ridiculous premiums for more than twelve years...on time, I might add. Now you're tellin' me I have to wait to git my check?" Bubba pulled up his pants.

"Maybe I can put a rush on the paperwork for you," the insurance adjuster said. "I'll see if I can't get my boss to take a look at those forms any quicker than that."

"Damn straight," Bubba said, "I've got me a business to run here."

"Yes, Mr. Gibson, we all do. I'm sure everyone just wants to do what's right."

After nodding, Merritt climbed into his car, then drove away. Bubba hitched his pants one more time. That idiot made him nervous...real nervous.

For the first time since he'd gotten involved in the whole mess, he experienced anxiety that he'd actually get away with it.

But hell, there was no way to trace it, he told himself again. Suspicions would always be just that. Suspicions. He'd been careful enough to make sure there was no proof.

He folded his arms across the bulk of his chest. Thirty days was a damned long time to wait on the money—especially since he'd gotten the check for the llama a whole lot quicker than that.

The chew tasted sour all of a sudden, so he spit it out in a single wad. At least the loan from the Southwest Bank had helped tide him over. Within a month, he could pay it back, and clear his other debts. Then maybe his wife would get those ridiculous notions out of her head and get her fanny back to the Flying Horse...where she belonged.

Bubba turned back toward the house. It was so quiet, so unwelcoming without Mary there. Mary's gentleness had helped him block out the morbid visions of the horses dying. Without her, his actions continually haunted him...and made him ill. Bubba knew one thing for sure; if he'd had it to do over, he'd have found some other way. Somehow.

As it was, he had to live with the crystal-clear memories for the rest of his life. And, for the first time, he wasn't sure he could even live with the future . . . or himself.

CHAPTER FOURTEEN

"WELL, WHAT DO YOU THINK, Nora?"

"That it's a bunch of coincidences that are ruining a dedicated man's career, that's what I think," she told Lynn, over a late-morning coffee.

"Agreed," Cal said, glancing across at his sister. Lynn took another bite of her muffin. "Until this, he's had an unblemished record. Lighten up, Lynn."

"But it's a scary position to be in," Lynn insisted.

"It's a scary position for Manny to be in, too," Nora said, refreshing the coffee, then putting the pot on the burner.

"Look, we talked about it last night at dinner," Cal continued. "If Daddy can support Manny, even after Bubba's been his friend for a long time, then you can, too."

"I suppose you're right."

Serena's hand wrapped around his thigh and squeezed. He placed a hand over hers before she got too carried away. After all, they were in a public place. He looked over at her. She mouthed, "Thanks."

But Cal was sincere. He believed in Manny's innocence without any encouragement from Serena.

"Daddy said he's not sure what Scott's going to do about his veterinary service," Lynn said.

"I'm going to talk to Scott later."

"When Bev picked up the boots for Jeff, she said Carolyn at the Circle T isn't going to jump ship, either," Serena supplied. "So Manny's still got support, even if it doesn't look good right now."

"I'm glad," Nora said, still including herself in the conversation.

"Say, Nora," Lynn began, "what do you know about Mary leaving Bubba?"

"Just that she felt she had to get away for a while."

"Do you know where she is?"

"Can't say I do, exactly."

"Did it have anything to do with Billie Jo Dumont?"

Nora shrugged. "She didn't say so, but a woman can only take so much."

Serena and Lynn nodded agreement.

"Hey, don't look at me!" Cal protested when all the women turned his direction. "I'm done running around."

"You're right about that," Serena said. "Don't count on me displaying the same kind of dignity Mary has shown."

Nora kept the rest of her conversations with Mary to herself.

"How's Tracey?" Nora asked Serena. "She looked mighty down when she was in here this morning."

"She still was when I stopped by the shop this morning." Serena toyed with her spoon. "I think she has pretty strong feelings for Manny, and she's taking this personally."

"No doubt about those feelings," Nora said with a chuckle. "It's written all over her face when she looks at him."

"Like these two here," Lynn supplied, glancing at her brother and Serena.

"As if you should talk," Serena teased.

Lynn blushed. "All right. So maybe I shouldn't."

"I'm gonna have to tell all the men in this town to stop drinking the water. It just isn't safe anymore," Cal said, then let out a painful burst of air when Serena's elbow connected with ribs that had been broken far too many times.

"Well I, for one, think it'll work out," Nora said. The three people sitting at the table nodded their agreement.

MANNY LEANED BACK in his chair, feet propped on top of his desk. He'd spent the entire day at Texas A&M, searching book after book, magazine after magazine, report after report. He'd dropped handfuls of dimes into the photocopy machine, copying pages he might want to read again. And he was still no closer to an answer.

Manny jumped when a crack of thunder ripped through the night air. The sky had looked threatening during the entire drive back from the university. Obviously, the fall storm had finally decided to wreak its havoc on the land. Drops of rain pelted the roof and the overhead lights flickered. But he wasn't ready to call it a night.

Grabbing a pen and a yellow pad, he listed—for what seemed like the twentieth time—all the circumstances as he could remember them. He jotted down dates and times that he'd seen the animals, and what his reactions and thoughts had been. Then he thumbed through the pages he'd copied, notes he'd taken while conferring with some of his old professors. There had to be a connection, somewhere.

The rain continued, escalating to a deluge now. Thunder clouds collided viciously, rumbling their anger. The storm was getting to him...making him restless. The lack of sleep was catching up to him, too. And so was the fact he hadn't held Tracey in his arms since early that morning.

Manny dropped his feet to the ground with a thunk just as the phone rang. Hoping it was Tracey, he answered on the first ring.

"Manny, it's Scott Harris." They exchanged pleasantries for a few seconds before Scott stated what was obviously on his mind. "Nothing personal, Manny, but I wanted to discuss the particulars of the incident at the Flying Horse Ranch."

Manny's grip tightened on the receiver.

"At this point, I have no intention of contacting another vet."

"Go on," Manny said flatly.

"But I have a responsibility to my animals as well as to my guests."

"If you want promises, Scott, I can't give them to you." There was silence at the other end of the line. "Unless I can find out what happened, why those horses and that llama died, I can't make promises."

"I see."

"I don't want to minimize the problem, but it appears to be an isolated incident."

"Nothing like this happened before I moved here that I don't know about, did it?" Scott asked.

Though Manny struggled to mask his anger, he had to admit that if he was in Scott's boots, or those of the other ranchers in the area, he'd sure as hell be concerned, too. "If you're asking if any other animals have dropped dead for no good reason while under my care since I've been here, the answer is no."

"That'll do for me," Scott said, and they ended the conversation.

Manny heard the door open in the reception area. "Hey, Manny!"

Recognizing the voice, he called, "In my office, Cal."

Cal entered Manny's office, his Stetson soaked. From under his rainproof jacket, he pulled out a slightly soggy copy of the morning news. "Did you see this?"

Manny took the newspaper, folded so his picture and the accompanying article showed. He read the article, then slapped the newspaper back down on his desk.

"I came by on behalf of the Double C to let you know we're standing behind you."

Manny rubbed the bridge of his nose. "Hell. This should never have been necessary," he said. "But I appreciate the support."

Cal took off his coat and hat and hung them on the wall pegs. The hat began a steady drip onto the tile floor. "It'll blow over," Cal said, dropping onto a chair on the opposite side of the desk from Manny. "People are going to find out it's damned inconvenient to call all the way to Austin in an emergency."

"I wish I could be as optimistic."

"Did you find anything out at A&M?"

Manny shook his head. "So far, it still looks like a strange coincidence. Their hearts stopped beating and the animals died."

"You giving up looking?"

"Hell, no."

"I didn't figure so." Cal stood and put his soggy Stetson back on. "Nasty weather out there," he remarked. "Drive carefully."

After Cal left, Manny locked up and finished the few items pending on his desk. Then he phoned Tracey to let her know he was on his way over.

He dashed to the truck, but got soaked anyway. Lightning flashed, in time for him to see where to insert the key in the lock. Within seconds, he was inside, with the heater switch on low. He reached for a favorite tape and slid it in the cassette deck while the engine roared to life.

The sound of rain and thunder filled the cab, in eerie consonance with the chilling weather outside. The opening strains of Garth Brooks's "The Thunder Rolls" swirled through the cab.

Manny drove a few miles per hour under the speed limit, entranced by the awesome display of lightning streaking out of the clouds toward earth.

He fumbled to turn up the volume of the music—hell, anything to escape the constant thoughts of the dead horses.

The thunder rolls . . .

Manny saw Flying Wind lying lifeless in the hay.

And the lightning strikes . . .

Manny's insides twisted. A flash of lightning sizzled toward the earth. Then it vanished, as if it had never existed. Rain slashed against the windshield, and the thunder cracked again. Several simultaneous streaks of electricity brightened the sky. Trees were silhouetted around him—black against black. From a faraway time, Manny remembered his *madre*'s warnings to avoid trees during storms.

He rewound the tape and started the timely song again. Strangely, the words haunted him.

And the lightning strikes . . .

Manny braked to a halt in front of Tracey's apartment, then shut off the truck's engine. He left the key in the ignition so he could listen to the concluding lyrics.

Involuntarily, he drummed his fingers on the dash as he sorted through vague snatches of memory. He remembered seeing a story on the front page of a tabloid at the grocery store several years ago, about lightning striking a racehorse just as he was about to cross the finish line. The jolt of electricity had traveled through the horse, killing both him and the jockey instantly. Their hearts had stopped, and the horse had fallen in his tracks. They'd never known what hit them.

Manny dropped his head onto the steering wheel as a sick taste choked him. Never in his life had an idea so heinous slapped him in the face.

And the lightning strikes....

Electricity. Heart failure. Electrocution.

¡Madre de Dios!

Manny dragged his fingers through his hair, pushing that errant lock back from his forehead. Hell. It couldn't be. It couldn't *not* be. Bubba had motivation, plenty of it. Several thousand dollars in insurance money was a powerful motivator. Everything made sense. Two and two finally did add up to four.

Manny shook his head and heaved a ragged sigh. Bubba had murdered his own animals, a llama and two beautiful, proud quarter horses.

But the damnedest thing was...it wasn't against the law for him to do just that.

BUBBA GAZED OUT the back window, able occasionally to see the stables by the flare of electricity in its purest form. He'd never hated storms...until tonight.

Though he tried desperately to chase away the memories, they came to him in snapshots. The next rushing in before the last one had even faded away.

He saw the machine. Heard the scared whinny of the animals. Heard his own lying, soothing words to the animals. Saw their knees wobble, then their legs collapse, heard them draw their last terrified breaths. Recognizing the enormity of his sin at last, Bubba Gibson hated himself.

Hell, it hadn't even been worthwhile. Mary still wouldn't come back. She called every once in a while, but refused to say where she was staying. And he'd heard from the insurance company that there'd been some sort of holdup, so they couldn't cut the checks sooner than thirty days from now.

The night was black. And his life had never been blacker.

"I NEED TO USE your phone," Manny said.

Tracey held open the door. "Come in." She took his hat and his coat. "You're soaked."

"Yeah," he said, reaching in his back pocket for his wallet. He dropped it on the table.

"Is everything okay?"

"No."

While he worked on getting his boots off, Tracey took his wet outer clothes into the kitchen. She sat his hat on the dish drainer and found a hanger for his jacket. Then she rejoined him in the living room, carrying a cup of hot coffee for each of them. "Manny?"

"I know how Bubba's animals died. And why..."

Tracey was alarmed at the dark tint of exhaustion beneath his eyes and the pale, nearly sunken look to his cheeks. She sat next to him, glad when he grabbed her and pulled her tightly into his arms. In seconds, she was as cold and wet as he, but she didn't care....

Beneath her ear, his heart pounded. "He murdered them, Trace."

She froze, though he continued to stroke one of his palms across her back. "Murdered?"

"When I heard about the insurance money, I guessed Bubba must have had them killed. His animals were worth more dead than alive. But I just couldn't figure out how." His nostrils flared in anger, and the muscles in his jaw rippled as he paused.

"As sick as it sounds, he electrocuted them. It's the only possible way it could have happened. There's absolutely no way to trace it unless you know what to look for."

She shivered in disgust at the thought, while Manny continued to massage her mindlessly. "Can you prove it?"

"Doesn't make any difference in a court of law how many animals he murdered. It's perfectly legal for him to do it."

She pushed away from him, not believing what he said. "What?"

"It's not against the law to kill your own animals. It's immoral, but not illegal. Insurance fraud is the only way we'll ever nail the sonofabitch."

Tracey's mind reeled at Manny's words. "Poor Mary. This is going to kill her."

"I've gotta deal with this right now," he stated. "Then I need to talk to you."

She looked at him.

"About us."

"Us?"

"Tracey, I haven't wanted to talk to you until this was completely behind us. But I can't wait anymore."

Tracey was shaken, but she struggled desperately to maintain her composure. "Make your call, Manny. I'll be in the kitchen."

He kissed her lightly, though she tasted promise in the way his lips lingered. As she left the room, her hands trembled.

Manny reached for his wallet on the table and pulled out Marvin Merritt's card. The whole incident was so insidiously grotesque, Manny knew he couldn't live with himself if he didn't report his hunch.

Thunderclouds rumbled again, and lightning caused the lights to go off for a few seconds. When the power returned with a buzz of electricity in the background, Manny yanked the receiver from its cradle and punched in the numbers.

Surprisingly, Merritt was still in the office. When Manny identified himself and stated his suspicions, Merritt swore.

"I thought he was out to squeeze money from us, but didn't have any way to prove it. Would you be willing to testify in court?"

"To what?" Manny asked. "We've still got no way to prove it. It's an educated guess, that's all."

"Maybe a bluff'd work."

"Maybe," Manny said doubtfully. "Not that I think my testimony would help any. But I'm willing to do anything I can to prosecute the man."

"You think he has an accomplice?"

"There's no way for me to say. But if he does, I doubt it's any of the ranch hands. The men I spoke with seemed innocent."

"There's no telling."

"I didn't figure Bubba for that type, either," Manny remarked with disgust.

"Hmm...I hadn't considered the possibility sooner...." The man's voice trailed off as the sounds of paper shuffling came through the receiver. "I'll bet I know who Bubba hired," Merritt mused. "I've been on the trail of a ring of animal hit men, but I've never been able to find out how they were killing the horses. I'm sure with the right incentives, one of them will talk. I'll take it from here, Mr. Hernandez. Much obliged to you for coming forward."

"I don't know if it helped any."

"It sure as hell didn't hurt," Merritt said.

Manny gave the adjuster his home number and address. After he hung up, he went in search of Tracey, anxious to hold her.

"I'm sorry you had to deal with this," Tracey murmured softly from her place near the window.

Lightning flared again, highlighting her hair and outlining her slender body. He was reminded of the time she stood in his kitchen, dripping wet, hair plastered to her scalp and jeans outlining every curve.

"It's a long way from over," Manny said carefully. "Unless Bubba gets a conscience all of a sudden and confesses, there's a good chance he'll get away with it."

A look of revulsion passed over her.

"There's no guarantee I can even clear my name. If this comes out and if Bubba denies it, it could actually make things worse."

He dug a hand into his back pocket. He'd never been in a situation like this before...wanting to confess his love but not having a clue in hell how to do it. "My reputation may stay in the mud, and it could drag my business down with it."

"It doesn't matter to me," Tracey said. "I've believed in you all along and I don't intend to desert you now."

"Tracey, you confessed once that you weren't very good at—" his voice lowered as he finished, "—making love. I appreciate now how difficult it must have been for you because this is one of the hardest things I've ever had to say to anyone." Manny ran the palm of his hand over the rough stubble of his two-day-old beard. Tracey's eyes were open so wide, so trusting. He didn't know how she felt or if she could ever love him even half as much as he loved her.

"I love you, Tracey," he finally blurted out.

A smile, tentative at first, then wider and more sunny, spread across her face. "I love you too, Manny."

"Look, I can't make any promises about our future here, can't swear that it'll be easy."

"Manny?"

He dropped his hand to his side.

"It doesn't matter."

She crossed the room to where he was standing. "I love you and I'll always love you, no matter what. I believed in you when you were beginning to doubt yourself. And I'll always believe. . . ."

Her words touched his heart. "We're going to have disagreements, if only because of our backgrounds."

"We'll have to learn to compromise."

He nodded. "And I'll have to work at coming to you, instead of staying away when I have difficulties."

"Tonight was a big step in the right direction," she said, reaching up to trail her small fingers down his cheekbone. "You didn't have to come here, but you chose to. That means so much to me."

"Marry me, Trace?" He caught her chin, desperate to see her face, read her expression.

"Is forever too short a time?"

"Hell, yes," he said, letting go of the breath clogging his throat with a huge burst. Smiling in triumph, he leaned down to capture her lips. "Too damn short."

She rose on tiptoe to meet him. He inhaled her scent, and let her words of acceptance unfurl in his heart. Though the lightning, rain and thunder continued to pound Crystal Creek, for Manny, the future couldn't have looked sunnier.

"Manny?"

"Hmm?" he asked, not letting go of her for even a second.

"Hold me. Make love to me . . . with me."

"*Querida,* I can't think of anything I'd like better." Manny scooped his future bride into his arms, holding her tightly against his chest. Her fingers threaded into his hair and her head settled lovingly against his shoulder. He'd never completely trusted a woman before. But now that he knew how fulfilling it could be, he vowed he would do anything to keep from breaking that incredible bond.

THE SCREAM OF A SIREN woke Bubba from a sound sleep. He wrapped his robe around his waist, then headed toward the stairs.

By the time he reached the bottom, someone was pounding on the front door. "I'm comin', I'm comin'," he hollered back. After turning on a lamp, he blinked against the much brighter light outside.

"This is the police. Open up!"

"What in the tarnation?" Bubba fiddled with the lock for a few seconds before releasing the mechanism. He yanked open the door. "Now what the hell are you wantin' with me in the middle of the night?" he demanded of Sheriff Wayne Jackson.

"I've got a warrant for your arrest, Bubba."

"You gotta be crazy," Bubba said, starting to close the door.

Wayne's foot stopped it from closing all the way. "Don't make it difficult on yourself, Bubba," he said, pushing the door open again.

"There must be some mistake," Bubba insisted. "Why the hell would you want to arrest me? I ain't never done nothin' wrong."

"There's an insurance agency out of Austin that disagrees. It seems a man named Lester Cain is more than willing to talk about names and dates. We already have a fella in jail who claims you hired him and agreed to pay him a percentage of the insurance money.'' The officer removed a pair of handcuffs from his belt and reached for Bubba's arm. ''I've got a warrant for your arrest for insurance fraud.''

Bubba saw the handcuffs glint metallically in the beam of the spotlight. Real fear, for the first time ever, careered through his heart. ''Come on, Wayne, you don't need those things, now do ya?''

''It's a formality, Bubba.''

He swore viciously and wished he had a wad of chew in his mouth. ''Well, hell, at least let me put some clothes on.''

''I'll wait.'' Wayne followed Bubba back inside. ''Don't be trying anything funny, now, Bubba. Let's not make this messy.''

Upstairs, Bubba took his sweet time getting dressed. A framed snapshot of Mary on his dresser grabbed his attention, and he picked it up. Did they let you have pictures in prison? ''Oh, hell, sugar,'' he said out loud. ''I made a real mess of things now.''

And he didn't even know where to reach her. As if she'd even care if he rotted the rest of his life in the Claro County jail.

Damn. He'd been found out. But he had to admit, a certain part of him was glad. He deserved to be punished. Hell, he'd been punishing himself already.

Knowing that if he took too long Wayne would start to get anxious, Bubba nervously hitched up his pants and headed down the stairs . . . to the waiting patrol car.

Wayne snapped the cuffs on Bubba—cold, impersonal metal against his warm skin. He fought the instinctive response to struggle; it wouldn't do any good. Even if he escaped, he'd still have his conscience with him.

Bubba was vaguely aware that Wayne was reading him the Miranda rights, but Bubba wasn't listening. He was in his own world, asking for forgiveness, wishing he'd never sunk so low in the first place.

"Do you understand these rights as I've read them to you?"

He nodded.

"I'll need to hear you say it."

"Yes," Bubba muttered. "I understand my rights perfectly."

Wayne helped Bubba into the back seat of the car, then slammed the door. As Wayne began to drive away from the house, Bubba wondered if he'd ever see it—or Mary again.

At least Mary would be pleased to know she'd been right all along. He had finally learned that his pigheadedness cost him all the things that were truly important.

MANNY NEVER KNEW how it happened, but news of his impending marriage to Tracey seemed to be common knowledge down at the Longhorn, even before he and Tracey arrived for breakfast.

After pausing to hear several congratulatory comments, he escorted Tracey to a table. The brand-new boots she'd given him, with deer hand-tooled into the sides, echoed off the time-worn floor.

"Did you hear Bubba Gibson was arrested last night?" Nora said, pouring two cups of coffee, one each for Manny and Tracey.

Manny whistled long and low.

Nora continued, her voice loud, as if she wanted every single person in the Longhorn Coffee Shop to hear what she had to say. "The sheriff came by after he got off work this morning and said Bubba was charged with insurance fraud in the death of those animals out at his ranch."

Manny felt a surge of gratitude toward Nora. Single-handedly, she was working to save his reputation. And she could do it in a day, where it might take him weeks, even months.

"Guess the warrant was issued around eleven o'clock last night. Wayne had him down at the Claro County jail by midnight."

Manny couldn't believe Merritt had moved so fast. Obviously, the man was a whole lot more powerful than Manny had originally believed.

"Wayne said Bubba might cop a plea bargain in return for testimony against the guy who actually did the dirty work. He was supposed to get ten percent of the insurance payoff. Not bad money for a few hours' work...that is, if you can live with yourself afterward."

Manny nodded. As much as he wanted to see Bubba suffer for what he'd done, it was important that everyone involved got taken out of the game. And Bubba wouldn't dare try anything like that again.

"Some of us never believed you were negligent, Manny," Nora said, smiling proudly.

"Hey, excuse the interruption."

Manny looked up and recognized one of the ranchers whose name had appeared in the newspaper as having dropped Manny as vet. Manny exchanged glances with Tracey.

"Don't cut off your nose," she said softly.

"Uh...I've got a calf who looks a little under the weather...." the rancher said hesitantly, uncertain of his reception.

"I'll be out right after breakfast. Unless it's an emergency?"

"No emergency," the man assured him. "Later this morning's soon enough."

Tracey grinned triumphantly.

"So how's Mary?" Tracey asked softly when everyone else was out of earshot. "Does she know what happened?"

It didn't surprise Manny that Tracey would think of the repercussions on Mary.

Nora dropped her voice. "I called her this morning. I figured she should know."

Tracey nodded.

"She was upset, naturally, but she told me she couldn't bear to see Bubba just now." Nora shrugged. "That man surely didn't appreciate what a wonderful wife he had in Mary."

Some people entered the café, and Nora headed toward the new arrivals. Manny relaxed against his chair and reached for Tracey's hand. She curled her fingers around his.

He glanced outside. On the way in he'd seen only a few lingering mud puddles as a reminder of the viciousness of last night's storm. Today, the sun shone and hardly a cloud hung anywhere in the blue sky over Crystal Creek.

Tracey squeezed his hand and he smiled back.

Justice had been served. And he had Tracey. Hell no. Life didn't get any better.

Relive the romance...
Harlequin and Silhouette
are proud to present

by Request™

A program of collections of three complete novels by the most requested authors with the most requested themes. Be sure to look for one volume each month with three complete novels by top name authors.

In January: **WESTERN LOVING**   Susan Fox
                                    JoAnn Ross
                                    Barbara Kaye

Loving a cowboy is easy—taming him isn't!

In February: **LOVER, COME BACK!**   Diana Palmer
                                        Lisa Jackson
                                        Patricia Gardner Evans

It was over so long ago—yet now they're calling, "Lover, Come Back!"

In March: **TEMPERATURE RISING**   JoAnn Ross
                                     Tess Gerritsen
                                     Jacqueline Diamond

Falling in love—just what the doctor ordered!

Available at your favorite retail outlet.

REQ-G3

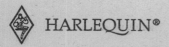

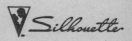

My Valentine 1994

Celebrate the most romantic day of the year with
MY VALENTINE 1994
a collection of original stories, written by
four of Harlequin's most popular authors...

MARGOT DALTON
MURIEL JENSEN
MARISA CARROLL
KAREN YOUNG

*Available in February, wherever
Harlequin Books are sold.*

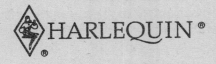

HARLEQUIN ®

VAL94

NEW YORK TIMES Bestselling Author

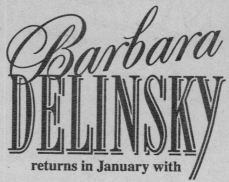

Barbara DELINSKY

returns in January with

THE REAL THING

Stranded on an island off the coast of Maine,
Deirdre Joyce and Neil Hersey got the
solitude they so desperately craved—
but they also got each other, something they
hadn't expected. Nor had they expected
to be consumed by a desire so powerful
that the idea of living alone again was
unimaginable. A marrige of "convenience"
made sense—or did it? BOB7

HARLEQUIN®

**Fifty red-blooded, white-hot, true-blue hunks
from every State in the Union!**

Look for MEN MADE IN AMERICA! Written by some
of our most poplar authors, these stories feature fifty of
the strongest, sexiest men, each from a different state in
the union!

Two titles available every other month at your favorite
retail outlet.

In January, look for:

DREAM COME TRUE by Ann Major (Florida)
WAY OF THE WILLOW by Linda Shaw (Georgia)

In March, look for:

TANGLED LIES by Anne Stuart (Hawaii)
ROGUE'S VALLEY by Kathleen Creighton (Idaho)

You won't be able to resist MEN MADE IN AMERICA!

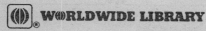

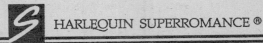
HARLEQUIN SUPERROMANCE ®

Women Who Dare will continue with more exciting stories,
beginning in May 1994 with

THE PRINCESS AND THE PAUPER by Tracy Hughes.

And if you missed any titles in 1993
here's your chance to order them:

Harlequin Superromance®—Women Who Dare

#70533	DANIEL AND THE LION by Margot Dalton	$3.39	❏
#70537	WINGS OF TIME by Carol Duncan Perry	$3.39	❏
#70549	PARADOX by Lynn Erickson	$3.39	❏
#70553	LATE BLOOMER by Peg Sutherland	$3.50	❏
#70554	THE MARRIAGE TICKET by Sharon Brondos	$3.50	❏
#70558	ANOTHER WOMAN by Margot Dalton	$3.50	❏
#70562	WINDSTORM by Connie Bennett	$3.50	❏
#70566	COURAGE, MY LOVE by Lynn Leslie	$3.50	❏
#70570	REUNITED by Evelyn A. Crowe	$3.50	❏
#70574	DOC WYOMING by Sharon Brondos	$3.50	❏

(limited quantities available on certain titles)

TOTAL AMOUNT	$
POSTAGE & HANDLING	$
($1.00 for one book, 50¢ for each additional)	
APPLICABLE TAXES*	$ _____
TOTAL PAYABLE	$ _____
(check or money order—please do not send cash)	

To order, complete this form and send it, along with a check or money order for the
total above, payable to Harlequin Books, to: *In the U.S.*: 3010 Walden Avenue,
P.O. Box 9047, Buffalo, NY 14269-9047; *In Canada*: P.O. Box 613, Fort Erie, Ontario,
L2A 5X3.

Name: _____

Address: _____ City: _____

State/Prov.: _____ Zip/Postal Code: _____

*New York residents remit applicable sales taxes.
 Canadian residents remit applicable GST and provincial taxes.

WWD-FINR

FLASH:
ROMANCE
MAKES
HISTORY!

History the Harlequin way, that is. Our books invite you to
experience a past you never read about in grammar school!

Travel back in time with us, and pirates will sweep you off your
feet, cowboys will capture your heart, and noblemen will lead
you to intrigue and romance, *always* romance—because that's
what makes each Harlequin Historical title a thrilling escape for
you, four times every month. Just think of the adventures you'll
have!

So pick up a Harlequin Historical novel today, and relive history
in your wildest dreams....

BE PART OF CRYSTAL CREEK
WITH THIS FABULOUS FREE GIFT!

The attractive Crystal Creek cowboy boot brooch—beautifully crafted and finished in a lovely silver tone—is the perfect accessory to any outfit!

As you share the passions and influence of the people of Crystal Creek...and experience the excitement of hot Texas nights, smooth Texas charm and dangerously sexy cowboys—you need to collect only three proofs-of-purchase for the Crystal Creek cowboy boot brooch to become YOURS...*ABSOLUTELY FREE!*

HOW TO CLAIM YOUR ATTRACTIVE CRYSTAL CREEK COWBOY BOOT BROOCH... To receive your free gift, complete the Collector Card—located in the insert in this book—according to the directions on it. If you prefer not to use the Collector Card, or if it is missing, when you've collected three Proofs from three books, write your name and address on a blank piece of paper, place in an envelope with **$1.95** (Postage and Handling) and mail to:

IN THE U.S.A.:
HARLEQUIN CRYSTAL CREEK PROMOTION
P.O. BOX 9071
BUFFALO, NY 14269-9071

IN CANADA:
HARLEQUIN CRYSTAL CREEK PROMOTION
P.O. BOX 604
FORT ERIE, ONTARIO L2A 5X3

Below you'll find a proof-of-purchase. You'll find one in the back pages of every Crystal Creek novel...every month!

PREMIUM OFFER TERMS

Requests must be received no later than March 31, 1994. Only original proofs of purchase accepted. Limit: (1) one gift per name, family, group, organization. Cowboy boot brooch may differ slightly from photo. Please allow 6 to 8 weeks for receipt of gift. Offer good while quantities of gifts last. In the event an ordered gift is no longer available, you will receive a free, previously unpublished Harlequin book for every proof-of-purchase you have submitted with your request plus a refund of the postage and handling charge you have included. Offer good in the U.S.A. and Canada only.

Here's a proof— of purchase— start collecting Today!!

ONE
PROOF-OF-PURCHASE

088-KAW

CCPOPR